Traumatized

A PORT CITY HIGH NOVEL

SHANNON FREEMAN

SADDLEBACK
EDUCATIONAL PUBLISHING

SADDLEBACK
EDUCATIONAL PUBLISHING
www.sdlback.com

ISBN-13: 978-1-62250-774-0
ISBN-10: 1-62250-774-6
eBook: 978-1-61247-985-9

Printed in Guangzhou, China
NOR/1014/CA21401594

19 18 17 16 15   1 2 3 4 5

ACKNOWLEDGMENTS

I have to first mention the families living along the Gulf Coast. People must think we are crazy to stay and brave the numerous storms that come our way. We follow closely as news unfolds about which way the storms are turning. We get in our cars and sit through hours of traffic, hoping that when we come back, our homes will still be standing. And year after year, we fight that good fight ... man vs. nature. No matter how bad it gets, we keep coming back to the cities that we call home.

To my readers, thank you for continuing this journey with me. This is the seventh book in the Port City High series, and if you are here, then you are all in with me. You are truly a part of me. You are the reason that I want to write. The reason that I work so hard to get the story right. I hope you love PCH as much as I do. It's my first series! It's been life-changing for me. But I want to ignite in you the fire to follow your own instincts. You may not want to be a writer, but you are going to be great at something. Listen to that still small voice on the inside, and run with vision. If I can do it, you can do it.

For my husband, you always have my back. Even in the toughest times, when I look at you, I know that everything is going to be okay. You are my foundation, my stability, my rock, and I am your rib. I love you, Pooh.

For my children: Kaymon, Kingston, Addyson, and Brance. I hope that my working this hard makes your life just a little bit easier. Doors will open for you that were closed to me. I am going to keep pushing, but know that you have to push too. You are all so gifted and talented. One day you'll know your own purpose as I have found mine. I promise you, as my mother did for me, I will help you make your dreams come true.

For my sister, Rochelle Jenkins, I love you, Rodie! When you were eight years old, you got on your knees and prayed for a sister, and there I was. I was the answer to your prayers, and you have always treated me as such. My love for you began before I was even born. You gave me three more people to love: Michael, Blake, and Dylan, who I have tried to make proud of their Auntie Shannon. Love you, Jenkins family … more than words can say.

For Felisha Collins, you are my sister. When we met in fifth grade, I had no idea that you would be with me until the end of time. You support my vision whenever and however you can. You look for opportunities to bless me, and it does not go unnoticed. I am blessed to call you my best friend.

For Shannon Richard, the other half of Shannon squared. Since we both raised our hand when Mrs. Hall was calling roll in fourth grade, you have been by my side. You have been the best, best friend. You are truly heaven sent.

Thank you, God! Thank you, God! This is an amazing adventure.

Thank you, Saddleback! I am a part of a team of people who I trust and who trust me. You had an ear to hear. You gave me a chance. You changed my life and the lives of my children, and quite frankly, my children's children. I don't think words can say how grateful I am, but I always try. I feel that you have to know what role you have played in my world. Again, thank you.

DEDICATION

To Carolyn Warrick, my mother. Through love, you have shown me the role of a woman in her household. Your love, support, and encouragement have led me to my dream.

TRAUMATIZED

Prologue

*O*n the first day of school, Shane, Brandi, and Marisa stood looking at Port City High School as if they were seeing it for the first time. It seemed a lifetime ago that they had arrived at PCH. Now, after all they had been through, they were still together.

"Our last first day of school at PCH," Brandi said excitedly.

"How can you be so happy about it?" Marisa asked. "We have had some good times here, and now it will be over in less than a year."

"Well, at least we have college. One

year at Port City College, and then we can go our separate ways," Shane said, taking a deep breath. "Right?"

"Yeah," Brandi and Marisa agreed with their best friend.

They had all wanted to go away to college, but they couldn't decide which university would meet all of their individual needs. They decided to stay in Port City for one more year and take their basic college courses together. One thing about Port City College that people from the area loved was the ability to transfer credits to larger universities. Knowing that, the decision to navigate through the first year of college together, instead of separately, had been a no-brainer.

"Look, we are on the last leg of the homestretch, and I'm ready to experience it all," Brandi told them. "And as head cheerleader this year—"

"I'm so sick of that phrase!" Shane fussed, turning to Brandi. "How many times have we heard that this summer? As head cheerleader this year," she said, mocking Brandi.

"Hey, I don't say it that much," Brandi protested.

"Well, as feature twirler this year ..." Marisa said, laughing, mocking her best friend.

"Can I quote you on that, said the editor in chief of the *PCH Gazette*," Shane said, holding a pen to Marisa's mouth as though it were a microphone.

"Okay, okay ... I'll stop saying it," Brandi groaned, rolling her eyes. "But ain't life grand? I love being a senior. We are gonna rule the school."

"Spoken like a true head cheerleader. Let's go before Brandi can't get that big ole head through the door."

"Shane! You know it's not like that. Seriously, who would have thought I would be head cheerleader? It usually goes to doctors' daughters or pastors' daughters, not, you know, girls from families with 'issues,' " she whispered, making quotation marks with her fingers.

"Shane's just kidding with you, B. You know we are happy for you. Nobody deserves the position more than you."

"Thanks, Mari."

"Yeah, yeah, what she said," Shane said playfully.

"Love you too, Shane. Now, let's go get our senior year underway."

They walked into Port City High School, and the first thing they saw was a huge wall display celebrating the new senior class's graduating year. Upon closer inspection, they saw a collage of pictures taken of their class every year since ninth grade.

Many seniors had congregated around the display, reminiscing about the previous school years. Some had tears in their eyes as they remembered all the great times they had at PCH, but others took time to laugh at their younger selves.

There was such a mad crush that Shane, Marisa, and Brandi had to wait for the group to clear out a bit.

"Oh no, look at my hair on that homecoming picture. Those bangs are awful," one girl said, laughing.

"I'm not much better. Look at my pants. I used to love those," her friend responded, laughing too.

"Good times," they agreed and headed to the auditorium. The seniors were scheduled to meet with the principal and their counselors.

Brandi and Marisa made their way through the crowd of seniors to see if their pictures had made it onto the wall. To their surprise, they were everywhere. "Look at how many pics we have on here. Somebody loves us. Shane, you have *got* to see these."

"I already did," Shane bragged, blowing air on her nails and shining them on her shirt.

"Wait a minute. You did this?" Marisa asked, confused. "When? We were together all summer."

"I have my ways," Shane told them. "I made this for our ten year class reunion. After this year is over, I'll make a separate board showing us all as seniors. Mrs. Monroe is going to have them all laminated for us. It will be awesome."

"No, it *is* awesome," Brandi corrected her. "I can't believe you did all of this, Shane."

When they arrived in the auditorium, there were several kiosks strategically placed on the stage, and lines of students had formed on the stairs leading up to it. This was the first year they were able to print their schedules, obtain information about their credits, and get recommendations on which college scholarships might be right for them based on their records. This was a much different registration than they were used to in the past. These were young adults taking care of their business. The girls fell into line with the rest of the seniors, eagerly waiting to see what their paperwork would reveal about their all-too-near futures.

As they looked around, they remembered back when they were freshmen. This same group of students had to be quieted numerous times when receiving their homeroom assignments back then. Now they moved like a well-oiled machine. What a difference three years made.

CHAPTER 1

Old School Rivalry

$\mathcal{T}$he football team gathered around and listened as Coach Davis lectured them on acceptable behavior during the week leading up to the big game with their all-time rivals, Riverdale High School.

Riverdale was founded right after integration in Port City during the civil rights movement. The white families who had been rich enough to leave, moved to the suburbs around Port City. Riverdale was one of the most attractive suburbs for former Port City residents. Since integration, the two towns had been competitors, and a natural rivalry formed between the two high schools.

Nobody knows exactly how or when "pranking" was added to the roster, but it became a thing when the two teams played against each other. Sometimes the pranks went according to plan, but there were those years where they went wrong.

On occasion, parents were called to the jail to pick their children up for trespassing or vandalism. Most parents didn't mind. Many of them had pranked Riverdale when they were in school too. Parents were more often upset by the failed prank than the fifty-dollar fines that accompanied the transgressions.

"Once upon a time, I sat in your seats as my coach lectured me on sportsmanship and taking the high road, but I didn't listen." Coach Davis told his story at the beginning of each football season. It was legendary in Port City—not many pranks had gone as badly as his. He wanted his team to stay clean.

During his senior year, Coach Davis was supposed to sign with a D1 university, but when a prank on Riverdale High went wrong, he landed in jail instead. It was big news for Port City, and it attracted the attention of the coaches on his future college campus. He lost his scholarship before he could put a toe on the field. He had to opt for a junior college instead, where he was injured during his sophomore year.

Matthew Kincade was the quarterback and captain of the PCH football team this year. He was at the center of the debate over whether to obey Coach Davis's wishes, or whether the team should make their mark by pulling the craziest prank yet. Matthew wanted the team to stay out of any controversy. He wanted the team to uphold Coach Davis's wishes so they could win state. Matthew looked at Coach Davis as a father. Many members of the football team did. The star quarterback tried to convince the team to listen to Coach. They could potentially win state this year, and that was more important than any silly prank.

"Coach thinks it's a bad idea. We need to listen to him if we want to make it to state," Matthew said to Jaylon Swanson, the running back for PCH.

Jaylon immediately became frustrated with the thought of doing away with pranking. "Man, stop talking about state. What's state got to do with those Riverdale punks? This game doesn't even count for state."

One of the other players jumped in between them as Jaylon stood up to get in Matthew's face. Jaylon had a hot head and became agitated quickly.

"J, just hear me out," Matthew yelled over the other players, who fed on aggression like a snack.

"You better talk fast," Jaylon said, trying to calm himself down.

"This is the way I see it," Matthew said, speaking to them as a group. "If we can come together on something positive, Coach will be proud of us. If we get busted because of a prank, we'll be in the doghouse. Let's not blow it over a stupid tradition."

"But it's a right of passage in Port City," Jaylon argued. "I took all of the hazing handed down by the seniors on my way into high school. Coach asked us not to go there this year, and we didn't. But no pranks on Riverdale? Come on."

"Just trust me, J. Me and you, we gonna take this team all the way to Austin. I'm telling you."

Jaylon reluctantly gave in, but not

without a disclaimer. "Just know if Riverdale strikes first, we striking back," he
warned, with his friends nodding in
agreement.

Brandi, Shane, and Marisa arrived
at school on Wednesday, and the atmo-
sphere was odd. When they pulled into
the students' parking lot, they noticed a
group of kids huddled around the flagpole
in the center of the lot.

"What's all the fuss about?" Shane
asked, quickly getting her camera out of
her bag.

They hurried out of the car and over
to the group of congregating seniors.
"What's going on?" Brandi asked one of the
freshman cheerleaders on the JV squad.

She pointed up. As if it had been
synchronized, Brandi, Shane, and Marisa
followed the flagpole with their eyes until
they were looking at the school's mascot,
a wildcat, hanging upside down by its four

legs. Of course it was a stuffed wildcat and not a live animal, but still ...

Marisa gasped. "How could they?"

As Shane snapped pictures, she was interrupted by the sound of Jaylon Swanson's car pulling up. His tires squealed against the pavement. He could be heard before he could be seen. "I knew it! It is *so* on now! This ain't right."

The crowd watched as Matthew Kincade walked over to him. "We still don't have to stoop, man. Just think about it."

"You think about it. We owe our fans more than this. PCH ain't never went out like this, and we are not about to now."

Friender was swamped with threats to the Riverdale Rebels. The Internet battle was heating up. That Thursday morning in Riverdale, people woke up to find the mile markers had been spray-painted. Everywhere it read Riverdale, the word "six" was close behind. Everywhere the mile markers said Port City, it read, "goes hard."

The city officials were livid. They were at PCH, questioning everyone. Nobody would admit to any involvement. The night of the game, police officers from Riverdale stormed into the PCH locker room, demanding members of the team be turned over. They showed pictures taken from video footage of three teenage boys who had vandalized public property: Jaylon Swanson, Mario Ruben, and Tyson Johnson.

"Oh no you don't," Coach said, stepping in between his team and the officers. "You aren't taking them anywhere."

"This warrant says we are."

"I know what you're trying to do, sir. I know what you are trying to do!" Coach Davis yelled.

"Sir, if you don't lower your voice, I'll take you to jail with your boys."

Everything in Coach Davis seemed to clench up. "Coach, don't," he heard Jaylon say. "We'll go with him. Tell my mom for me, please. You know people known to get lost in Riverdale."

"You don't have to worry about that," Coach assured him, looking at the officer. "You all just be quiet. Don't talk until your parents get there."

CHAPTER 2

Brandi

$\mathscr{N}$ews spread quickly about the three football players who had been carted off to jail by Riverdale police officers. The PCH fans were devastated. Brandi knew she would have to keep the crowd cheering for the team. She wanted the team to feel the support of their fans. They had to regroup.

Coach quickly changed their starters. The PCH team fumbled through the first half. During the halftime show, the cheerleaders went to meet the Riverdale cheerleading squad as they did for each game, but the other cheerleaders didn't meet them at the gate. Instead, there were police officers there.

"Excuse me, Officer, we were about to go to the other side."

"Nobody's going anywhere," the officer informed them.

They were confused. They had never been denied access to the other team.

"Sir, I'm the captain of the cheer-leading squad. Is there a reason that this is happening?"

"Yes, we were told by the head River-dale cheerleader that you all sent threatening messages over Friender. The pictures were sent to the police chief."

"What? We never ..."

She looked at her phone and saw the posts from her Friender page, stating that they would pay if anything happened to anybody on their football team. Her eyes refocused. She hadn't written those messages, and nobody had access to her account. The whole thing was baffling.

"Look, Miss, whether you did it or not, we have to treat it as though you did. You will not have access to the other team, and if our investigation proves that it was you, measures will be taken."

"What kind of measures?"

"It was a threat. You figure it out."

After the game, Brandi's plan was to stop home, change clothes, and meet Shane and Marisa for a stroll at the seawall. When she arrived at home, her parents were in the kitchen in a deep discussion.

"I can't leave, James. The hospital says that they need me."

"Well, we need you too. We don't know how long we are going to be gone."

"I tell you what. Let me help them get through the storm, and I'll meet you in Austin."

"Austin?" Brandi asked as she joined them in the kitchen.

"Oh, hi, baby," her mother said, standing up nervously.

"What's going on, Mom?"

"There's a storm in the Gulf. It looks like it's heading right for Port City."

"You need to go get yourself packed," her dad informed her.

"Are you kidding me? I was about to go out. We just finished whipping up on the Riverdale Rebels."

"Don't be silly, Brandi. We are under a hurricane watch, and you are worried about going out tonight?"

"Yes, I am. Do you remember what you did your senior year when y'all played Riverdale?"

"Do I? Me and my girls—"

"Exactly," Brandi cut her mother off.

"I get it, Brandi, but there wasn't a hurricane in the Gulf either. Grow up!"

"I heard you say that you're staying here. Well, I'm staying with you," Brandi said, looking for an out. Being crammed in a car for the next five hours was not how she wanted to spend her evening.

"Baby, just stop!" her mother screamed. "Look, we are under a lot of pressure. This is a big storm. They are comparing it to Katrina already."

"That wasn't that big. It was just their seawall wasn't strong enough. Port City won't have that problem."

"Keep knowing everything, little girl, and you won't learn a thing," her father scolded. "Now go get your things packed, and I don't want to hear another word about it."

She packed as much stuff as she could cram into her suitcase. There was always eeriness to packing for a looming storm. Nobody ever knew if they would see their home again, much less their belongings. After Brandi was done packing, she looked back at her room one more time. She took out her tablet and snapped a picture. "I'll be back," she told her things and closed the door to her bedroom.

CHAPTER 3

Shane

*B*randi sent Shane and Marisa a text stating that her family was on the road and heading to Austin. She told them to warn their own parents about the storm.

Mr. Haywood had been one of the first people informed about the hurricane's trajectory. He worked for the refinery, and they were usually the first to know. They were ordered to move out of the city quickly so if they needed the workers to come back, their families would be safely settled, eliminating worry.

Shane knocked on the door to her

parents' bedroom, but her mother stopped her from coming into the room. "Hey, baby. Daddy is on a business call. What do you need?"

"The Haywoods just evacuated. Should we be leaving too?"

"That's what they are talking about on the call. We will let you girls know as soon as we figure out what we want to do."

"Shouldn't we have a say so in what we are going to do?"

"If you would like. We'll talk as soon as Daddy hangs up."

Shane went into her sister's room. She had to warn her. "Robie, you up?"

"Kinda," she said groggily. "It's after eleven."

"I know, but we may have to evacuate tonight. There's a storm headed our way," she whispered, trying not to wake her nephew up.

"Shoot," Robin said, getting out of bed and heading toward the family room.

They sat in the family room, patiently waiting for their parents to explain what was happening. All the other times they had to evacuate, they had been little girls. All they had to do was get in the car. They enjoyed being at the shelters and meeting new girls from Port City and sometimes the surrounding towns. The kids didn't have a care in the world, but the grown-ups stayed glued to the TVs as they monitored the storm.

It was much different for them now. Shane worried about her car, which her father had purchased for her. She knew that if anything happened to that car, it would be a while before she got another one. Robin worried about Aiden and being stuck in traffic for such a long time with a toddler. They each sat, hoping their father was going to tell them the storm had turned.

When their parents entered the family room, they knew something was happening, and it wasn't good. "Look, a storm is coming," their father said. "It's headed straight for Port City and should arrive in about forty-eight hours. That means that it's coming onto land Sunday night."

Their father laid out the facts and their options. They could evacuate as they were instructed to do by the fire chief, or they could stay at the shelter provided for city employees. The Highland Hotel was the highest point in the city, hence the name, and had served as a makeshift shelter during many hurricanes.

"I don't want to get in that traffic with Aiden," Robin complained. "I vote that we stay here."

"Yeah, Daddy, and if the storm does turn, we will be right here in town. That's the plan. I vote for the shelter too."

"What do you think, Kim?" he asked their mother.

"The Fosters stay together. Gavin is

welcome to stay with us too. Then his mom will have more room in her truck."

"Yeah, I feel a lot better," Robin said, getting up to call Gavin. "I'm going back to bed now. When do we have to move into the shelter?"

"Sunday after church we'll start packing up."

"Okay, well, I'm going out," Shane told her family.

"Are you crazy? There's a storm coming and you're going out?"

"It won't be here until Sunday and today's Friday. Don't wait up!" she said, grabbing her keys.

CHAPTER 4

Marisa

*A*s she read the text, Marisa's body immediately tensed up. She was already dressed to go out with her girls, but Brandi was in the car heading to Austin. Marisa was aware that evacuations were always a source of conflict in her home. Her parents hadn't mentioned anything about the storm yet. She knew she should tell them, but that just meant an argument would start tonight instead of in the morning.

She opted to go out, enjoy the night, and face the fight in the morning. They were already in bed anyway. There was nothing they could do now.

"Hey, mamacita," Shane said, greeting her friend. "Your parents didn't think you were crazy going out when the storm's coming in?"

"I didn't tell them that a storm was coming in."

"What do you mean? You didn't tell them? Y'all have to get a plan together. You are crazier than me."

"You know how this is going to go in my house. Dad doesn't want to leave. Mom does. Dad wins."

"True. Mister M hates to evacuate," Shane said, "but I don't blame him."

"Look, we all hate it, but his decisions aren't rational."

As they rode through town, it wasn't bustling with students like it usually was on a Friday night. They headed to the seawall, where they knew they would find some of their friends, but it was deserted.

They got out of the car to get some fresh air. It was unusually cold for September. The waves beat violently against the rocks. The waters lapped against the seawall— its levels visibly higher.

"We better get outta here. This is kind of scary," Shane admitted.

"Yeah," Marisa agreed, looking at the water as it collided with itself. "It looks like we are the only fools out in this weather."

By the next morning, the news reports started coming in about the traffic on the interstate. After what she saw the night before, Marisa wasn't surprised that many Port City families had already started to evacuate. The Maldonados stayed glued to the television as Mrs. Maldonado tried to convince her husband to leave. He stood over a fresh pot of soup, letting the aroma guide him to a happier place. He had fresh radishes, cilantro, and limes cut as garnish. Normally they were all excited about his homemade soup, but they were all too antsy about the storm to enjoy it.

As Marisa and her siblings watched their normal Saturday morning lineup on television, an alert appeared on the screen listing the towns under mandatory evacuation. Port City was among them

"George, we have to leave. There won't be enough resources here." Her mother pleaded with her father for hours after they were put on the mandatory evacuation list. Finally, after what seemed like forever, Mr. Maldonado gave in.

As they frantically threw clothes into their suitcases, they were just happy that their father finally listened to reason. The last thing they wanted was to be stuck on top of their roof. It had happened to some people once before in Port City many, many years ago, and the Maldonado kids didn't want history to repeat itself.

CHAPTER 5

Exodus

By the time the Maldonados were packed and ready to go, the gas stations had run out of gas. There were rumors that five pumps on the outskirts of the adjacent town still had gasoline. Mr. Maldonado sat in the car, fuming. They were stuck in traffic. It would take an hour to navigate through the sea of cars to get to a gas station that still had gas. Once they made it to the station, there was no guarantee that gasoline would still be available.

"Let's play a game," Romero told his

sisters. They had already been in the car for over two hours and had not left the city limits yet. In fact, they had just completed a circle around the city and wound up back on their own street. All because of the search for gasoline.

"No games," Mr. Maldonado snapped.

"George," Mrs. Maldonado said, looking sternly at her husband.

"*Qué pasa?* I have to focus, Lupe."

When they got to the gas station, there was a line of five cars ahead of them. The frustration level grew with every minute. People were getting out of their cars and stretching their legs.

Their stories were similar. They had all been riding for hours and hadn't made it but five miles from their homes. It was looking as though it was going to be a long day. As their father pumped gas, their mother listened to the AM news and traffic stations in the car.

"The interstate looks like a parking

lot," a reporter on the radio announced. "It looks as though there was an accident. If you are still in a mandatory evacuation area, you should take an alternate route. For alternate routes, please visit us online."

"What are we going to do, Mama?" Marisa asked, concerned. She knew that her father was going to explode, and she was right.

From the open window, Marisa's dad said, "I'm going home, Lupe. We will just have to ride the storm out."

"We will do no such thing, George."

"At this rate, the storm will be here before we leave the city limits. I'd rather be in the comfort of my own home when that happens."

Marisa looked at the sky as her dad continued to pump gasoline.

Her mother sighed deeply. There was no reasoning with him at this point. Mrs. Maldonado looked back at her children. Those Maldonado eyes looked back at her.

The kids were afraid. Marisa could hear her mom praying quietly for her husband to listen to reason.

Brandi sat glued to the television as images of Port City panned across the screens of all major television news stations. Geraldo Rivera had just arrived in Port City. He was interviewing residents who were stuck in traffic or trying to get gasoline. He was also speaking with the stubborn people who refused to leave their homes.

When Brandi saw Geraldo at the Highland Hotel, she knew Port City was in more trouble than she had imagined. She tried frantically to reach her mother, but her cell phone was out of service. When she tried to reach Shane and Marisa, she received a similar response on their phones.

"Bran, come walk with me to the buffet. I'm hungry," Raven said.

She pulled herself away from the TV to take her little sister to the foyer, where a buffet was set up for breakfast, lunch, and dinner. It was part of the package her father had chosen. It was a good idea, even though he was not the type who ate much. But Brandi and Raven had inherited their mother's love of food.

All the televisions were tuned to news stations. Hurricane Adam was the topic of the day. And the nation was riveted, since this was the first storm of the season. Adam was growing in intensity every minute as it crossed over the Gulf of Mexico.

"It's not looking good for Port City," one older man said, standing up from his table.

"Thank God Austin is not even close," the server said as she poured him another cup of coffee.

"Bran," Raven whined, but Brandi shook her head at her sister.

She leaned down and whispered, "Don't let them scare you. We've been through this before. Everything will be just fine."

"But Mom, she should have left town with us."

"Your mama has been taking care of herself since she was eighteen. She grown." Brandi skillfully mimicked her mother. Raven laughed. She had taken her sister's mind off the storm. But Brandi was also stressed out. She wished she had someone to calm her down.

Worse than no gasoline during a hurricane was no supplies on hand. The stores were out of everything, and Mr. Foster was not prepared. He had been in the city all day with other council members, making sure things were in place as the storm approached. There was so much to be done, and they were running out of time.

By the time he got to the hardware

store to buy the necessary items to secure his own home, the shelves were bare.

"Ma'am, do you know where I can get some plywood?"

"Sir, the whole city is sold out of plywood, kerosene, and bottled water." His eyes panned the store in panic as the realization of her words sank in. She had to be wrong. His wife was going to kill him. He tried every store on the way home, but nobody had any inventory.

"Shane! Robin! Let's go!" he yelled as he ran into the house.

"We're coming, Dad. Gosh!" Shane yelled, balancing all of the belongings she wanted to take with her.

"What are you doing with all that stuff?" Her father scrutinized her piles of luggage.

"Hurricane Adam is supposed to be brutal. I'm just bringing the stuff I can't live without," Shane said.

Robin threw two suitcases down the

stairs. Her own and a small one for Aiden. She was carrying Aiden on her hip.

"Robin! Why are you throwing your suitcase?" her mother asked, balancing her own five bags.

"I'm holding Aiden."

"That child can walk now. So let him walk."

"We can't fit all of this stuff in the truck," her father fussed at them. "Where do you all think we are staying? We are going to be jam-packed in the hotel room with the six of us—including Gavin—as it is."

"Isn't it a suite?" Shane asked naively.

"Yes, a tiny one," Mr. Foster said. "Robin has the right idea, and she packed for two. You and your mother need to leave some of that behind."

"But, Brian," her mother whined, surprised at her husband's lumping her packing excess in with their daughter's.

He stopped both of them with the look on his face.

"Ah-ha," Shane said, teasing her mother as they consolidated their suitcases. "You got in trouble too."

"Shane Renée."

"I know, Mom, not the time to play."

CHAPTER 6

Marisa

*O*nce they filled the truck up with gasoline and were ready to head back home at their father's insistence, Marisa and her siblings were almost shaking. Yes, they had weathered storms before, but this one seemed different. The horror stories of families who hadn't evacuated from incoming hurricanes were well-known in cities along the Texas Gulf Coast.

The radio announcer gave them a storm update. "Many have been praying that this storm would turn, but it looks like it is still heading right for Port City. We think it will hit land by tomorrow. Citizens of Port City are being urged to evacuate." Her father turned the radio off.

"All of this overreacting about a storm," he mumbled. "Do you know how many hurricanes I have lived through?" he asked. "And look at this ridiculous traffic!" he snarled.

Nobody dared to answer him. Storm season was a stressful time in Port City. Many families were going through this same drama.

"Daddy, I bet if we make it to Houston, I could call my agent, Marcie Miller. She could really help us out." Marisa would have said anything to get out of town.

"We don't need help, Marisa. I have this under control," her father snapped at her. Just as he finished talking, something in the truck popped. The truck stopped dead in traffic.

"What was that?" her mother asked.

Smoke began to billow from under the hood of the truck.

"What now?" her father asked with a heavy sigh. He popped the hood. People began to frantically honk their horns as he got out of the truck.

"What do you think is wrong, George?" her mother asked as he tried to reach their personal mechanic.

"I think it's the engine. I can't get it to turn over. I'm calling Luis to come check it out." He called and called the mechanic, but there was no answer. Their truck blocked the flow of traffic trying to get onto the interstate. With the engine dead, it started to get hot inside. And just when they thought it couldn't get any worse, a police car pulled up behind them.

"Sir, I'm going to have to ask you to move to the side of the road so that the other cars can pass. We have to get the whole city cleared out," the officer informed the Maldonados.

Mr. Maldonado took a deep breath, got out of the vehicle, and with the help of a couple guys who came to assist, pushed their truck to the side of the road. Mrs. Maldonado sat in the driver's seat, steering.

"What do we do now, Papa?" Isi asked her father.

He didn't respond.

"I'm calling an emergency vehicle to come and pick you up," the officer said. "They will take care of you. Take only what you need out of your bags."

The children began layering their clothes as much as possible before the emergency vehicle picked them up from the roadside. They didn't know where they were being taken, but they were happy to be rescued.

The emergency truck drove through traffic with its lights flashing. *Now this is the way to evacuate,* Marisa thought.

"Where are they taking us?" Nadia questioned her older sister.

"I really don't know, Nadia," Marisa said with a sigh.

They pulled up to the Port City airport next to a small plane. It looked like a commuter plane, but Marisa wasn't sure. They were asked to board. So the entire Maldonado clan picked up their belongings and got inside.

When they entered the plane, there were already families seated and waiting. They were the last to board, apparently. There were no seats together. They each found a seat and strapped themselves in for the ride.

"I ain't never flown befo'," one old lady told Marisa.

Marisa reached over and patted her hand, which looked as though it had seen its fair share of sunny days.

"I'm sure we'll be fine. They should tell us where we are going shortly."

The plane doors closed and the fasten seat belt sign lit up. The passengers had no idea where they were going, or how long they would be there. As soon as the doors closed, the plane began to taxi. When it got into position for takeoff, it practically flew down the runway. The passengers groaned as the wheels of the plane left the ground. A couple nervous people were praying.

"Don't take me now," one woman moaned.

"Let me out. Let me out," one yelled.

One lady quietly prayed with her rosary beads. The Maldonados looked at each other across the plane. They didn't know if they should be frightened or relieved. The anxiety level was definitely high among this group.

They flew for over an hour, looking out the window, wondering where they would land. When the plane's wheels touched the ground, the pilot came over the intercom, "Welcome to San Antonio. We hope you enjoy your stay." The passengers cheered as the plane taxied to let them out.

"We made it," the little old lady said, patting Marisa on the hand this time. "First time for everything." She lifted her cane into position and prepared to exit the aircraft.

CHAPTER 7

Brandi

*H*i, Mama!" Brandi and Raven said, waving at their mom on the computer screen.

"How are my babies doing?" Catherine Haywood said, smiling back.

"They are fine, honey, but we miss you," the girls' father responded.

"Don't you worry about me. I'm in the safest place in Port City. This hospital was built to last. I'm just happy that the three of you are out of harm's way. Are you enjoying Austin?"

"We can't have fun, Mama. We are so worried about you," Raven whined.

"Look, you go see Austin. Explore the city and the University of Texas. Call some friends. Whatever will be, will be. I'm going to take a nap now. I have to be at work in a few hours."

"Okay, Mama. Love you," Raven told her.

"Love you too. Love you, Bran and Daddy. You all be careful out there. Come home in one piece."

"We will! Bye!" the sisters said in unison. It was hard to imagine their mom on her own during the storm, but Catherine Haywood was one tough cookie. The residents of Port City needed her more than her family did right now.

Raven took out the Skip-Bo cards and talked her sister into playing a game with her. They played cards and watched television until their stomachs needed food. They headed downstairs to see what there was to eat at the hotel's buffet.

When they were done with the surprisingly tasty food, the last thing they wanted to do was return to that cramped room.

Brandi decided to get on a city bus and take a ride through Austin. Raven was always ready for an adventure. They sent their father a text and let him know where they were headed.

There was so much to see in Austin. They kept their faces glued to the window. When they went downtown, the bus took them past the governor's home.

"Is that someone's house?" Raven asked her sister. "Who lives there?"

"The governor," Brandi said, almost drooling at the impressive estate. "I wish we could go in. I would love to see the governor's mansion."

"Me too."

They rode a while longer, looking at the interesting people getting on and off the bus. Their plan was to continue riding the bus until it made it back to their hotel.

"Last stop!" the bus driver yelled.

"What? Aren't you going back to the Comfort Way?"

"No, ma'am. This bus doesn't go past the campus. I'm off duty now. I have to bring the bus back to the bus barn."

"Bran, what are we going to do?" Raven looked at her sister fearfully.

The intensity in Raven's face made Brandi a little nervous. "Sir, I can give you extra money."

"I'm sorry. I can't. But don't worry. There's a bus coming along soon that will take you back. Or you can catch a taxi."

"Thanks," Brandi said. Reluctantly she got off the bus, holding Raven's hand.

They sat down on a bench and waited for another bus to come so they could make it back to the Comfort Way Hotel before nightfall. Luckily, it was still daylight saving time, but it was getting dark earlier and earlier. Brandi thought about calling her father, but she knew it would mean an endless amount of questions if she ever decided to venture out again.

Brandi only knew one person who lived in Austin, Erick Wright. Last year they had forged quite a bond while on the debate team together. He was very outgoing and handsome, but her long list of failed relationships had her defenses up when it came to love.

She had thought about calling him when she arrived in Austin, but she didn't know if he would want to hear from her, a little high school girl. She knew when people left for college, the last thing they wanted was their high school life squirming its way back into their new world. She never wanted to be *that* girl, but her options were limited as the time ticked away.

She took out her cell phone and dialed his number. "Well, hello stranger," he said, answering on the first ring.

"Hey, E. Did I catch you at a bad time?"

"Nah. I'm just catching a quick bite with a friend."

"Oh," she said sadly, picturing him with a beautiful blonde or brunette after his brief dip in the chocolate pond.

"What's going on with you? How's the family? I'm going crazy being all the way over here while Hurricane Adam is heading toward Port City."

"Where did your family go for the evacuation?"

"They are still trying to get here. To Austin. They made it to Katy, but had to stop there. Where are you?"

"Hang on a second," she said. All of a sudden with a little click, she was staring at Erick. "Hey," she said, smiling. Then she pointed her phone at the UT campus and panned the area.

"No way! You're here? Wait. I know exactly where you are. Don't move!" She laughed as she watched him stumble over his chair to get out of the restaurant, which looked like it came out of a University of Texas campus life catalog. She caught a glimpse of his eating companion, who looked like he would be a friend of Erick's, a mix of smart and cool, just like him. She was relieved it wasn't the girl of his dreams.

Brandi sat back down on the bench next to Raven, and they watched as students hurried past them to get to their evening classes. "Is this where you are going to be next year?" Raven asked her sister as she watched the busy activities of campus life.

"No, RaRa. I'm not leaving for another year, but after that, I hope so. I like it here."

"I do too, but I don't want you to leave me." Raven had tears on her cheeks. "I can't imagine me without you."

"You'll be just fine. I'll come home all the time. I promise. Please don't cry. You're going to make me cry."

Luckily, Erick found them before the

Haywood girls lost it and let their emotions get the best of them. He ran over. As he got closer, Brandi stood up automatically to meet him. He squeezed her tightly, and her feet left the ground as he picked her up in his arms. He did the same to Raven, who was just as happy to see him. "How did you get here? I know you didn't brave that Austin traffic."

"No, not quite. We were tired of being in the hotel, so we got on the city bus, but this was the last stop, so—"

"So you didn't really come here to see me. You got stranded."

"Don't make it sound like that."

"Well, it's true."

"I didn't want to bother you. That's all," Brandi said, studying her feet. "I know that you probably have—"

"Been wishing that fate would deliver you to me ever since the day I laid eyes on you," Erick said with a grin.

"That's not what I was going to say," Brandi said.

"But that's what you should have said. Come on, let's walk through the campus. I can show you around and get Raven some of the best frozen yogurt Austin has to offer. It's on the way to the student parking lot anyway. Then I'll drive y'all back to your hotel."

They ate their frozen yogurt in the student center and enjoyed a glimpse into college life before heading back to their hotel. When they pulled into the parking lot, Brandi sent her dad a text letting him know that Raven was on her way up to the room. She decided to sit in the hotel lobby and talk to Erick before heading upstairs.

"I wish that you would have called me yesterday. We could have had more time together."

"Erick, you can't tell me that none of

UT's cute girls has piqued your interest. Please. I mean, what do you want with me?"

"Why is your guard always up, Brandi?"

She looked out the window of the hotel as they sat in the lobby, trying to avoid his gaze. "I'm a work in progress, Erick. I don't think you want to put in the amount of work it will take."

"It's the best job I could ever hope for," he said, turning her face to his. Then Erick kissed her. Right there in the lobby. He kissed her like he had wanted to for a long time. "When the time is right, we'll know. I'll be right here, Brandi. No pressure."

She pecked him on the lips as she touched his cheek. "I know." She didn't know what she did to deserve him, but she was happy she did it. Whatever "it" was.

CHAPTER 8

Shane

The Foster family set up shop in their hotel room and braced themselves for the long night ahead. Nobody knew what to expect. The storm started as a tropical depression near Africa. By the time it was in the mid-Atlantic region, it had grown into a tropical storm.

The people along the Gulf Coast watched the Weather Channel, willing the storm to turn and not enter the Gulf of Mexico. By the time they watched Hurricane Adam cross the Bahamas as a Category 4, all news stations urged those along the Gulf Coast to keep a close eye on the storm's direction.

It looked as though many towns were on hurricane watch, and it would inevitably hit one of those Gulf cities. The whole nation watched when Category 4 storms demolished cities and towns. The most infamous, of course, being Hurricane Katrina. Hurricanes could be devastating.

When Adam met up with land in the Bahamas and Cuba, it lost some intensity and was knocked down to a Category 3. The cities under hurricane watch breathed a sigh of relief, happy that Adam was losing strength.

Locked away in the shelter with her parents, Shane found it hard to avoid the ceaseless play-by-play of the storm. It was on every channel in Port City. Shane tried to avoid the news with her tablet, but the signal was too weak, overloaded by users.

"I need to get some air," Shane said, trying to escape their small hotel room.

She took a deep breath when she got outside. She looked at her phone. It was six o'clock in the evening. Adam was set to hit land in approximately three hours. The skies were still fairly clear. *Please don't come to Port City.*

Shane made a quick decision. She needed to do something normal. So she decided to walk to a convenience store to buy a snack. But she was greeted by a sign hastily written with a Sharpie that read, Everything Sold Out. *Never seen that before,* Shane thought.

She made a beeline for the store across the boulevard when she saw patrons hurriedly rushing out of its doors. Trying to kill time, she leisurely crossed the street, preparing to rummage through the picked-over snacks. When she got to the door, she saw Christina, one of Brandi's friends from the cheerleading squad the year before. She was in her first year at Port City College.

"Chris? Hey!"

"Hey, Shane," she said glumly.

"Why are you still in town?"

"We got stuck here. My mom's job just released her to evacuate, but it's too late. We just went to the civic center to secure a cot and thought it best to come grab some snacks."

"Well, at least we are in town together. Do you still have my number?" Shane asked her.

"Yeah, I have it."

"Well, call me. We can hang out after this whole thing blows over. I'm sure we are the only two still here."

"You don't think the town's going to get trashed?"

"Do you remember the hurricane that blew through here in elementary school? Our parents were running to the school to get us out. We had one rainy night, and that was it."

"Yeah, but global warming—"

"We are going to be fine. Don't worry. Call me."

Shane was happy Christina was in town. She made her think of Brandi. She received a small signal on her phone, so she sent Brandi a message on Friender. There was no way of knowing if it had gone through, but at least she'd tried. Marisa hadn't responded to her e-mail either. Shane didn't know what to think.

Shane prayed for their safety, got some snacks, and headed back to the hotel room. She was so bored. She was ready for the storm to come and go. When she got back in the room, her family stood around the television as the hurricane trackers began to come to the same conclusion. Hurricane Adam was headed straight for Port City, Texas.

CHAPTER 9

Engulfed

The calm breeze had been blowing through Port City started to change quickly when night fell. Those not already tucked away inside a shelter felt the increasingly cool wind that the monstrous storm brought their way. They watched as gray clouds replaced white clouds.

"The storm is on its way," the fire chief said, looking out over the horizon.

"They say this one is going to be a doozy. Sure do hope ole Hurricane Adam is kind to li'l Port City, but I'm thinking we are going to make history tonight." His shirt was embroidered with the Port City logo and read "Bob, PC Electrician."

"We are ready for whatever ole Adam sends our way," the chief replied. He sounded confident that their city could withstand this storm.

"We are gonna have to be. We have seen Category Three storms in the area, but never Category Four, and this bad boy is a four again."

Shane ran back into the hotel and away from the cold wind, which only moments ago had felt like angels were blowing kisses directly toward her. Now that wind felt evil and eerie. *Something bad is about to happen. I just know it. We should have left. We should have evacuated!*

She doubled over next to the elevator, holding her stomach. She felt as though she couldn't catch her breath. No air was coming in as she took small, short breaths, gasping for air.

The elevator dinged and her father was

by her side. "Shane?" he said. He'd never seen his daughter like this, and he jumped into action to care for her. "Let's go find someplace quite where you can sit down, baby. Come on." He took her through the lobby of the hotel, with its restaurants and bars. The crystal chandeliers flickered.

The lobby was full of small groups of people. Shane could hear their conversations as her father hurried her away from their anxious voices. They were all talking about the fast-approaching storm.

Shane's father brought her into a quiet lounge area, free from bystanders.

"Just take a deep breath. Look at Daddy." He tried to coach her through what looked to be a panic attack. "Okay." He took a deep breath himself before moving on. "What's wrong?"

"I was outside, and the air started to change." She was still attempting to fully catch her breath. "These two men started talking about the storm, and I don't know what came over me. I just had to get away from them, but I couldn't breathe. I don't know." She shook her head, not knowing what just happened to her.

"It looks like you may have had a panic attack. You have nothing to be afraid of, Shane. We are all together. Daddy will keep his family safe."

She knew he would. No matter what happened tonight, she knew her father would never let anything happen to them. They walked back toward the elevators. She took a deep breath as she pressed the button for the seventh floor where they were staying. Her father had managed to secure a second room, so she stopped by Gavin, Aiden, and Robin's room to urge them to join her in their parents' room as the rains started to come down.

When they didn't immediately agree, Shane ran to her parents' room. Her journalism training kicked in, and she began documenting the approaching storm.

Everyone looked at the ceiling as the rain grew louder and louder. It sounded like golf balls were being thrown against the hotel by someone angry at the building or the people inside. It sounded deliberate.

"Daddy, what's that?" Shane asked, looking ten years old again.

"It's hail. Call your sister and tell her to get over here with Aiden and Gavin immediately."

Just as the hotel phone was in her hand, an icy ball of hail came crashing through their window. They gathered the few belongings they could as papers and receipts began to fly around the room. With the window broken, they could clearly hear the storm. Its howl sounded like a wounded animal crying.

"Go! Get out of here," her father yelled as he grabbed his briefcase and clothing. With a piece of the window shattered, it was only a matter of time before the whole thing blew in on them. They quickly left the room and shut the door firmly behind them.

They knocked frantically on Robin's door. It looked as though the hallway hadn't been touched by the storm's force, so they decided it was best to stay there until the hurricane passed. Robin, Gavin, and a screaming Aiden soon joined them.

Soon after, the mayor came out of his own room, wet and shaken. He joined them in the hallway. Robin returned to her room to get him a towel.

The hail and the wind had seriously damaged one side of the building. It felt like a nightmare as they watched friends and coworkers scramble for safety. And just as abruptly as it started, the storm stopped. The people in the hotel began to cheer, but the celebration was short-lived. In the distance, they heard what sounded like an approaching train. The sound grew louder and louder every second. Someone yelled, "It's a tornado!"

Those just leaving their rooms joined the others in the hallway as they crouched down and covered their heads. The tornado's winds began to blow out the remaining windows on their floor. They could hear the glass shattering behind the rattling doors of the abandoned rooms.

At that point, those in the hallway wanted even more secure shelter, so they all ran toward the stairwell to take cover. There were no windows there.

They began to breathe a bit easier when it seemed that they had found one safe place inside the hotel. Soon they heard what sounded like a stampede coming up the stairs.

"What is it?" Robin asked, looking to Gavin for answers. Gavin clutched a frightened Aiden in his arms.

City workers and news reporters from the lower levels greeted them. There was water in the hotel. Shane's eyes went to her father's before she began to run up the stairs. They had to make room for those on the lower floors as the water began to rise rapidly. It was utter chaos. First the hurricane, then the strong winds of a tornado. What was coming next?

How was the rest of the city fairing? Those seeking cover in the hotel felt like sitting ducks. There was no information coming in or going out.

Shane took Aiden from Gavin and held him tightly to her, rocking him and calming him down for the first time in hours. "I knew we should have evacuated." She was sweaty and tired. With no electricity, the temperature in the stairwell was warming up by the minute.

"It's hot, Daddy," she told her father. "We have to do something."

"It sounds like the worst may be over—" but before the words could escape his lips, Port City's warning whistle blew.

Shane studied her father's face. "What is that whistle for?" she asked. She felt her body tense up. Prior to that moment, she didn't think it was possible to feel any more tension.

"It's the seawall. There was a breach."

"What?" Robin asked in disbelief.

"It means—" he started to say.

"We know what it means. Don't scare the girls, Brian," Mrs. Foster said, not believing that they could be living through something so terrifying.

He grabbed his wife by the arm so that she would understand what was happening. "Look at me, Kim. This is serious. The whole town could flood."

The mayor met Brian Foster on the fifteenth-floor stairwell. "I need you to come with me."

Mr. Foster turned to his wife, who nodded her approval. Decisions were going to be made, and made quickly. Port City was experiencing the worst possible outcome. That whistle was *the whistle*. Brian Foster wanted to kick himself for not evacuating his family when he had the opportunity.

"Daddy, don't go," Shane whined, looking up at her father.

"He has to, Shane. Now stop," Robin told her sister.

The news that the Highland Hotel had flooded hooked television viewers from around the country. People were fixated by the disaster and the crazy reporters who were covering it live on national TV.

Nobody would discover until later that two people had already drowned in the hotel's basement, where a pipe had burst during the tornado and the strong winds that came with the hurricane. Surprisingly, the flooded hotel and the seawall breach were totally separate events.

The old historic hotel had taken a beating during the storm. Witnessing the destruction was a little like watching a horror film. The crazed killer knows exactly where his victims are and does everything in his power to destroy them. Hurricane Adam was a monster of a different sort.

Brandi and Marisa found a signal and were able to Facetime from their respective locations. They both watched as Geraldo Rivera told of his near-death experience in Port City when water began to gush into his room, which filled up like a fishbowl.

"Why hasn't she called?" Marisa asked as she watched the terrifying nonstop account of the storm. "Can you believe the water destroyed the seawall like it wasn't even there? Gosh, the whole town looks like it's flooded."

"I know. This cannot be happening. Shane's probably busy doing stuff like trying to stay alive. I don't know, though. That's just me thinking that."

"Brandi, you're scaring me even more."

"Shane is going to be fine. Haven't you met her?"

"Yes, but—"

"No buts. She'll be fine." Brandi willed herself to believe it. "She is fine. She is fine." She wanted Marisa to believe it too. She put on her brave-girl face, but she knew the videos Port City residents were posting online were downright frightening.

She was happier than ever to be sitting in a hotel room in Austin. If only she knew how Shane was, she could enjoy it a little more. News about the hospital where her mom worked wasn't available either. She was worried sick about her mother, but she was sure nothing could be as bad as the Highland Hotel.

CHAPTER 10

Marisa

Marisa couldn't sleep. She lay on her cot in the San Antonio evacuation center, watching one of the televisions turned to CNN. She watched as Anderson Cooper stood next to the heavily damaged Highland Hotel, reporting on the state of Port City. Many of the homes in the area were underwater, making it very difficult to get into town.

Helicopters flew over Port City. The waters had risen the highest in this coastal town. She could see Lakeview, where Brandi had been found two years ago when she was rescued from her kidnapper. The entire area was submerged. The lake had overflowed. Rescue workers were checking all flooded homes. The National Guard was maintaining order. And the Army Corps of Engineers attempted to drain water from low-lying areas.

The helicopter flew over an area she recognized. It was near the seawall where homes used to be standing. Strong waves had beat against those homes for hours. The historic mansions in that area had been preserved for years. Some had been turned into charming bed and break-fast hotels for tourists. Hurricane Adam had reduced many of them to rubble in a matter of hours.

Marisa sat up in her cot. She walked toward the television. She couldn't believe her eyes. "*Mi hija*, are you okay?"

It was like she was in a bad dream. "Mama, what if our home is gone? What will we do?"

"We will survive, Marisa. We've seen our share of tough days. It'll be hard, but we will survive."

"When are they going to take us home? How are we going to get home?"

Now that the storm had passed, there were so many unanswered questions. Nothing about this experience was normal.

She wanted to run from the shelter, but she didn't have anywhere to go. They had been to all the tourist destinations in San Antonio. There was only so much fun you could have when you were stranded in a strange city with no transportation and a hurricane threatening to destroy everything that you loved.

"I want to go home too," Isi said to her mother. She was ten years old and getting more mature by the minute. You saw in her both the emerging young woman and the young child still not left behind.

Marisa looked at Isi's long legs, much like her own. They had inherited their body type from their grandmother, who was rumored to have some German in her, but she was just *abuelita* to them.

"Look at what you are starting, Marisa," her father scolded. "Now we will play the cards we were dealt."

"That's easy for you to say, Papa. It's your fault that we are in this mess in the first place. If only you had listened, we could be in Austin with the Haywoods. You ruined everything!" She ran out of the shelter and into the hot, dry San Antonio air. She began to cry.

As fate would have it, the little old lady who sat next to her on the plane appeared by her side. "Don't cry," she said, gently rubbing Marisa's hair. "It's gonna be okay." Her presence startled an already annoyed Marisa. She couldn't even cry in peace. When she saw the little old lady, her whole demeanor changed.

"Have you seen the news yet? It is *not* okay."

"Did someone in your family die, baby?"

"No, ma'am. It's just Port City ... it's destroyed."

"And it's been destroyed before," she said matter-of-factly. "I remember it like it was yesterday. Now, don't you go worrying 'bout Port City." She laughed. "It's going to be just fine ... just fine."

"It's been destroyed before?"

"Oh, yes. This isn't the first time that the sea turned on us. I was about your age. We didn't have shelters like this with the fancy flat-screen televisions." She laughed at the memory. "We all crammed into the gymnasium on the black side of town. At that time, we weren't even allowed in the civic center. It was the whites only shelter," the old lady sighed.

"Needless to say, we didn't have much. The night Hurricane Judy came in, we lost what we did have." Her eyes had a faraway look to them. "Those waters came in that night as we frantically pulled the bleachers down, trying to climb to higher ground. I was a frightened young girl, and I watched as people I knew lost their lives in that gymnasium. But when it was all said and done, we came together as a community, and we rebuilt homes, grocery stores, dry cleaners, and we did it with our own hands. I tell you, we have a lot more machines and help now than we did back then."

She looked at Marisa with a serious face. "Port City will be just fine, honey. Don't you worry your pretty little head about Port City. It's strong, and its people are too." She patted Marisa on the hand, stood up with the help of her cane, and walked back into the shelter.

"Thanks," Marisa said, knowing that she probably couldn't hear her. She was feeling much better after their conversation. She walked back to their area of the shelter and straight to her father. "Papa, I'm sorry. I should not have disrespected you like that."

"It's okay, mi hija. We are all under a lot of pressure right now." He watched as the news crews got closer to their neighborhood.

"Dad, that's our street!" Romero exclaimed, trying to get a better view of the condition of their neighborhood.

"Anderson Cooper is on our street," Mrs. Maldonado said in disbelief.

They hung on his every word. "You can see the awesome destruction here. This side of the street was flattened by a tornado. Amazing weather conditions, folks. The hurricane birthed the tornado. We believe it produced winds of one hundred forty miles per hour."

It was their worst nightmare come to life. "Thank God we weren't at home," Mr. Maldonado said, rubbing Isi's head and looking at his children in disbelief. "This could have been bad."

"Tornadoes can be the deadliest part of a hurricane," Anderson Cooper announced. "But look with me at the other side of the street. Here, not one home was damaged. It looks as though they weren't even in the storm. This is very common when dealing with tornadoes. We will be keeping a close eye on the unstable weather. More tornadoes are likely, due to the tumultuous conditions here in Port City, Texas. Back to you in the studio."

None of them said a word. Their home was still there. Their pictures, belongings, everything still intact. They were even able to see their garden. It had seen little to no damage. It was a miracle.

Mr. Maldonado turned to his family with tears in his eyes. "Let's pray." The relief they felt was overwhelming. Now they just had to find their way back home.

CHAPTER 11

Brandi

As Brandi watched the news from her hotel room, her thoughts were with her mother. She hadn't talked to her yet and was worried sick about her. She had gone down to get breakfast with her father and sister earlier, but the smell of food nauseated her. She couldn't eat until she heard from her mom. The longer it took Catherine Haywood to call them back, the more worried Brandi became.

"What do you think she's doing?" she asked her father.

"Saving lives, like your mama does. It's her gift."

"Well, we need to get home. We need to check on Mama."

"I've been on hold with FEMA all morning, getting our FEMA numbers and instructions for our next move. Right now, they aren't letting anyone back into the city. It would be easier for her to get to us, but you know she's not leaving that hospital."

They tried to reach neighbors and family who hadn't evacuated to make sure they were okay. When Mr. Haywood was able to reach his brother, he told him about the nightmare they had survived.

"You think you know what it's like, but, man ..." He took a deep breath, trying to find the right words. It had been a long time since Mr. Haywood had heard his older brother get choked up. "They got us living like savages out here. No running water, no electricity. It's bad, bro."

"Man, is there anything that I can do?" Brandi's dad asked.

"Nah, they're going to get us back up and running. It won't be easy, but I'd rather be here in Port City than anywhere else right now," his brother replied.

"Good. Well, I'm here if you need me. If you hear anything about Cat, will you let me know?"

"Of course, baby brother."

The news about St. Augustine's Hospital was slowly beginning to trickle out to the public. News stations began setting up outside the hospital as they described the grim scene there. There had been multiple deaths. The hospital had been in the tornado's path. Patients could not be transported away in time. And worse, some generators had failed. The news could not have been worse.

"No," Brandi gasped as she frantically dialed her mother's phone number. There was still no answer.

Her father went to take a shower. The room was starting to smother them. There was nowhere to go ... nowhere to clear your head.

Brandi couldn't stop calling her mom. She was pacing around the room. Then she went into the hallway of the hotel. *C'mon, Mama, pick up.*

"Hello? Hello?" her mother's voice was hoarse, urgent.

"Oh, Mama," Brandi said as she made her way back to her hotel room. The last thing she wanted was for her call to drop. "Are you okay?"

"I'm fine, baby. How are you all?" Brandi could tell that her mother was crying. She had heard that voice enough in her lifetime to know.

"Raven, it's Mom," Brandi hissed.

"It's Mom?" Raven sat up. She had already imagined the worst and was thankful that her mother was on the phone. Tears slid down her cheeks from the relief she felt. She ripped the phone from Brandi's hand. "Mama, when will you get here?"

"Soon, baby. You being good?"

"Yes, ma'am. You sound funny. Why do you sound like that?"

"I'm just a little hoarse. We were trying to talk to one another over the sounds of the storm. I love my girls. I need to go now. Tell Daddy to call me, please."

"We love you too, Mama," they both screamed through the receiver.

Their mother was so strong. Hurricane Adam had been a monster of a storm, and Brandi couldn't imagine what she had gone through. It must have been intense. The most important thing was that she was still here. *Thank you, God.*

CHAPTER 12

Shane

I can't sit in this room any longer," Shane told her family.

"It's dangerous out there, Shane," her mother warned her. "People are looting and carrying on. You need to be right here with us."

"We've been here for five days now. I can't take it anymore. I just want to get some pictures of the debris before everything is cleaned up."

"I'll go with her," Gavin volunteered. "I could use a little air myself."

There was no food left in the hotel.

They had been living off of rations for two days now. It was the only thing that FEMA had been able to get in to the residents of the Highland Hotel. It seemed like a feast once the rations arrived. Everyone was ravenous.

"Are your eggs green?" Shane had whispered to Robin.

"They look just like yours, Shane."

"I can't wait to leave this place. I'm moving inland for college. No more hurricanes for me."

"Don't talk like that, Shane," her mother scolded. "We've been through enough. I can't imagine you far away from me."

Shane couldn't sleep in the hotel another night. She had thought about what she would do when this craziness was over. There was only one logical answer to her: California. She had loved it there, in the land of no hurricanes. She was deathly afraid of earthquakes, but decided that anything was better than what they had lived through. She didn't want to share her decision with her family yet. She didn't even know if she could make it through a year of college in Port City. At this point, she was ready to jump out of her skin.

When she and Gavin stepped outside the hotel doors, they looked at the devastation all around them. They could see looters as they ransacked stores and businesses. Shane took out her camera. These pictures were priceless. You didn't wake up every day with America looking like an emerging nation. Port City had been declared a disaster area. People were coming in from across the country to help.

"We don't need help. We can clean this up ourselves," Shane sniffed.

"Don't be silly, Shane," Gavin replied. "We need help. Look at our town." It was like being in a bad dream. It was hard to put into words the feeling you got when you could see devastation in every direction.

Mr. Foster had taken a boat ride

around the city the day after the storm. Many areas were still underwater at the time, and he had returned to the hotel very depressed. He had been by their friends' homes. Some had been destroyed by the tornado, some still had water in them, but their home had suffered little damage.

"I feel guilty," he had confessed to his wife. "We were very lucky."

The mayor's home had been totally destroyed because the tree in his front yard had come down during the storm, collapsing the home's roof. His family's belongings had been scattered all over the neighborhood. One of the other city council members had lost everything too. It was a hard time for Port City.

Shane got as many pictures as she could. "I'm gonna go up closer to the damage," she told Gavin.

"No, you're not."

"Gavin," she said sternly. "I'm going there. Are you coming or not?"

He took a deep breath. "Well, you know I'm not letting you go alone. You are a stubborn girl, Shane Foster."

They descended the hill but were stopped by the National Guard when they got to the bottom. "Where are you two headed?" one of the officers asked, holding his gun across his chest.

"I was just going to get some pictures. I work for our school newspa—"

"Nobody's allowed out without a pass from the mayor, and I don't see a pass."

"We'll head back, sir," Gavin said nervously.

"No we won't. You can't tell us what to do. This is our city."

"Miss, your city isn't the city you know. There are snakes, alligators, and looters here right now. This is in your own best interest. Now, head back up where it is safe."

"I don't want to go back there!"

"Officer, we are sorry. I'll take her

back up," Gavin told him. "Shane, pull it together. This will be over soon."

She started to cry. "Not soon enough, Gavin."

When she returned to the room, they were surprised to be able to get Internet service. It was a little bit of normalcy during a crazy time.

The first thing Shane did was hook up the video chat. She called Brandi and then Marisa. Soon they were all on the conference call.

"Are you okay, Shane?" Marisa asked.

"Not really, Mari. It's worse over here than you could imagine. Daddy went by your homes. There's not too much damage. We all came out okay, but I can't say the same for the rest of Port City."

"I actually saw my house on CNN," Marisa said.

"No way. We are on the map like that?"

"Have you seen my mom?" Brandi asked.

"No, B. There's no way to see anybody. Some GI Joes just stopped me when I tried to leave the hotel. It's crazy here. When are y'all coming back?"

"When they let us," Brandi told them.

"I'm still stranded in San Antonio," said Marisa. "We don't even have a way home. We go out walking a lot, and we went to the Alamo yesterday."

"Well, that's fun," Shane said, feeling a bit envious.

"Yeah, but there are only so many times you can go to the Riverwalk. I just want to come home."

"We don't really have a home right now," Shane told her. "Be happy you are there."

"Our money is getting low," Brandi whispered. "I don't even think we can afford to stay here any longer." She didn't want her dad or Raven to hear her. "I just pray our FEMA vouchers kick in soon. Mama tried to come and meet us, but she didn't make it. Got as far as Houston. I think we are going to try and get closer to Port City soon."

"Good, I miss y'all."

"Hey, I have to go now," Marisa told them. "FEMA just got here with information. Love you both!"

"Love you too!" they said in unison.

CHAPTER 13

After the Rain

It had taken a week, but residents were finally allowed back into the city. Some gathered the few belongings they could salvage and left town, while others made the decision to tough it out in Port City shelters. This put a bigger strain on the resources. There were more people in need of water, food, and generators.

Overall, the residents wanted to stay home and start rebuilding. If they could find enough food, supplies, and fuel, they could stay in their own homes and start the long cleanup process.

The refineries were back up and running, and the workers were called and told to return to work. This meant that the Haywoods could count on the refinery for their basic needs. They were given an emergency supply kit: a generator, bottled water, and army rations. It was more than others had, and they were grateful.

Shane and her family were able to move back home, but they had to live on the second floor for now. The water in their neighborhood had risen just enough to damage the flooring on the first level of their home. The carpet would have to be pulled up, but the hardwood floors had escaped with little damage.

Although Mr. Maldonado had already found a job in San Antonio, Marisa's family had been ecstatic when FEMA came in and issued bus vouchers for those families that wanted to return to Port City. With newly acquired supplies to take back home with them, the journey had been hard on the cramped bus. Most people had taken everything donated to them. They had all heard the stories about people who had returned without basic supplies, and the difficulties they faced in trying to get them.

It didn't matter how much money a person had, they couldn't buy what wasn't there. So the Maldonados sat on the bus, balancing whatever they could to aid them in their journey. They didn't care about the horror stories. They just wanted to get home.

It was harder than they imagined. The city was barely functioning, but the surrounding cities had pitched in to help.

By Saturday, electricity had been restored. There was a town hall meeting scheduled for that evening. Everyone attended, hugging friends who were there. Many residents had not returned home for one reason or another, but the faces at the meeting were those who were determined to return Port City to normal.

The mayor began to speak. He praised the workers for their ability to get the city up and running as quickly as they did. He listed all of their accomplishments over the past week. "It has been a challenge, and we still have many challenges ahead. Please know that we are trying. Nonetheless, I speak to you today with a heavy heart."

The mayor took a deep breath. "Port City High was damaged to a point that we will not be able to open it back up on time." The crowd murmured loudly, and the mayor attempted to calm them. "Wait, please. This is hard on all of us. Students will have to enroll in other school districts right now. Riverdale has been kind enough—"

"Riverdale?" someone yelled from the crowd.

"Boo," the people started to yell.

"Come on, Mayor!"

He tried to calm them down. "River-dale is the closest high school. We have bus access there, and FEMA has already started putting trailers in the back of the school, where we will hold classes. We have to do this. We don't have a choice."

"Homeschool!" someone yelled.

"That is your decision. I can't make it for you. Please, look at this as a temporary setback. Our students will return to PCH."

The crowd was in shock. The students cried, especially the seniors. They let their tears fall for their lost identity, their lost city, and their lost senior year.

The three girls went to Brandi's house after the town hall meeting, exhausted. "This is awful," Brandi told her friends as they rested in her room. "I'm not going to school with those Riverdale fools. I'm just not."

"It's our senior year. Nobody should have to do this," Marisa complained.

"They're our biggest rivals, and now we are going to be in trailers in the back of their school. It's just not right."

"Look what they are calling us on Friender, the Refugees," Shane said, appalled, turning her tablet around for them to see. "I hate Riverdale."

"How can we be refugees in America?" Brandi asked, jumping up. "See, I can't do them. I'm homeschooling for real."

"Riverdale students are just mean and spoiled rotten. They always have been. You know I don't do mean, and they feed on it. Ugh!" Marisa screamed out of frustration. She buried her face in her hands in an attempt to pull it together.

"Okay, I'm not homeschooling," Shane told her friends. "I can't. There's too much going on at my house. Aiden would never let me get any work done. I have to feel inspired. I don't like it, but I have to go to Riverdale, and you two can't make me go alone."

Marisa and Brandi searched each other's faces. They always had each other's backs, but this was a bit much. "Come on," Shane whined. "Let's just look at it as an adventure. New school, new boys," she said, nudging Brandi.

"Ooh, cuties ... now you're talking my language," Brandi said, smiling for the first time since the town hall meeting.

Marisa looked at Brandi and rolled her eyes. "You gave in way too fast."

"What can I say? She's persuasive," Brandi drawled.

Shane was excited that her friends were now on board. She began planning right away. "Okay, so this means we have to get us right. They can call us refugees, but we don't have to look like refugees. It is time to beautify. Let's get out of here. We need hair, manicures, pedicures, and some super fly clothing. No way I'm showing up at Riverdale High torn up. No way!"

"You act like we have beauty shops

up and running, Shane. We barely have water," Brandi lectured.

"B, we drive. Let's hit up Baymont and make this happen. FEMA didn't send us checks for nothing. We have to spend them," Shane said convincingly. Each person who had been displaced by the storm had received a check—children and adults. It was a drop in the bucket compared to everything they had lost, but it helped.

Marisa laughed. "You are *so* right. My parents gave me my money yesterday. I haven't spent a penny."

"Exactly."

"Say no more. Let's roll!" Brandi exclaimed.

CHAPTER 14

Brandi

Brandi looked everywhere for her mother. But she could not find her in the house. She wanted to show her all her new clothes that she bought with her FEMA money. She peeked in the garage. Her car was there, so she had to be home.

She sent Raven a text asking where everybody was. Raven wrote back that she was on the way to the movies with their dad. Now Brandi knew her mother was somewhere in the house.

She went to her parents' bedroom and found her mother on the floor in her closet. Her legs were pulled tightly to her chest, and she was crying.

"Mama, what's wrong?" Brandi startled her mother. Catherine Haywood must have thought she was alone in the house.

"Brandi," she said, wiping away her tears. "What are you doing here? I thought you were shopping with the girls."

"I was, Mama. Why are you crying?"

"I'm okay. It's nothing for you to worry about. Now, show me what you bought." She stood up and joined Brandi for a sneak peek at her purchases. "I like everything you bought, Bran. You are going to look beautiful. You okay with going to Riverdale?"

"No, but I'm going to make the best of it," Brandi said with conviction.

"Good girl," her mother said proudly.

Brandi could tell that something had changed about her mother, but it was hard to put her finger on it. She had heard the horror stories about the devastation that they witnessed on the night of the storm, but her mother refused to talk about it. She said that she wanted to put it all behind her. But it didn't look like she was doing that. Brandi wanted to help her mother, but she didn't know how.

When Raven and her father returned from the theater, she asked her dad if she could speak with him privately.

"What's up, Brandi?" he asked.

"Have you noticed how Mom's acting?"

"Mom had a rough night when that storm came in. You saw the news. You know what happened at the hospital."

"People died, right?"

"Yes, but it was a little bit different this time. It was a lot of people, and some were under your mom's care. It wasn't right."

"Did she tell you that?"

"No, she won't talk to me either. I've asked some of the people I know who work there. She was the go-to, so she took on a lot of the hard jobs that night. Just give her some time, Brandi. She'll be okay."

"Okay," she said reluctantly, "but it's already been two weeks since the storm. How much time do we give her?"

"However much she needs. You hungry?"

"Yeah, I saw you picked up pizza," she said, smiling. Her mother and sister were already at the table. Her mother was laughing and talking with Raven like she didn't have a care in the world. *Okay, maybe she will be fine. Everybody has to cry it out once in a while,* Brandi thought.

CHAPTER 15

Shane

When Monday morning finally arrived, it felt like the first day of school all over again. Shane nervously dressed in the new clothes that she purchased over the weekend. She knew that she was looking her best, but her stomach was still doing flips.

While she waited for Brandi to pick her up, she scrolled through Friender. She knew it was a bad idea. She shouldn't want to know what kids were saying at Riverdale, but it was like a moth to a flame. Surprisingly, the Riverdale students were involved in their own drama. When one of the Riverdale cheerleaders made the comment that her parents were going to homeschool her if they couldn't count on the school to keep the PCH kids separated from the Riverdale kids, Friender went nuts.

"Do you know what they've been through? It could have easily been us."

"Put trailers on their own campus!"

"Y'all are mean ... smh."

"Go back to the hood," one student wrote.

Shane heard Brandi outside and grabbed her purse. "What's wrong?" Brandi asked when she arrived at the car.

"I don't want to go."

"You are the one who got us hyped up to go. Are you serious right now?"

Shane detailed the arguments and read the comments to her from the Riverdale students. By the time they pulled up at Marisa's house, they were both angry.

When Marisa got in the car, they filled her in on the drama. "So you don't want to go?" she asked them both. "There's no way that a couple of ignorant students will ruin our senior year. Let's grab some coffee and take this ride to Riverdale."

"Mari, just one day off. Let them work out the kinks, and we can start tomorrow."

"No," Marisa said, shaking her head. "We go today. We are the head and not the tail. They will not decide our future. We do."

"Ooh, look at you, feisty," Brandi said, looking at her friend through the rearview mirror.

Marisa had to laugh at herself. "I've been listening to inspirational sermons. They got me pumped up this morning."

"I see," Shane said.

"Hey, there's a Just Joe coming up on the right. Pull in, and I'll treat to some coffee," Marisa said.

"Three caramel macchiatos, extra

caramel and whipped cream on top," Brandi yelled in the drive-thru speaker.

"Um, no!" Marisa yelled. "I won't fit into my twirling costume. Make that a nonfat, no whip, white chocolate mocha for me. And a banana. Please."

"I need comfort food," Brandi said as she pulled the car toward the window.

"You see I didn't change my order," Shane said, laughing.

As soon as they pulled away, Brandi opened her sunroof and turned on the Young Dub song that she had been listening to before her friends got in the car.

"Young Dub's not banned from getting play anymore I see," Shane yelled over the music. Brandi had fallen for Young Dub at a very vulnerable time in her life, but he had not been the person she thought he was. When he cheated on her with another rapper, Lil Flo, she was devastated. Time had started to heal those wounds. Just being able to play his music without becoming angry showed that she was getting over it.

"Girl, Lil Flo even has a verse on here, but the song's so hot that I can't help but jam to it."

"I am not mad!" Shane said, dancing along with her friend.

Marisa sat in the back, taking in the scenery. There were ships moving along the port. Some hunkered down low in the water, indicating that they were filled with the black gold that Southeast Texas was known for. Barrels of oil were being shipped all over the world. The amount of money that the area took in was unimaginable. Not that the citizens near the Gulf were getting a piece of the pie, but the tax dollars benefited Port City's infrastructure and beautification, to the point that made other cities envious.

"This is too far to go for school," Brandi complained right before Riverdale High School came into view.

"Riverdale is nice in the daylight," Shane said.

There were signs directing the PCH students to the back of the campus. There were breakfast trucks and welcome signs. There were supply trucks for students who arrived without proper clothing.

"Well, this isn't what I pictured at all," Shane said as they exited their vehicle. She put her cup of coffee on the roof of the car and began to document their arrival at Riverdale.

"Well, at least they know how to make us feel welcome. I could get used to this," Brandi said. The football field was right next to their classroom trailers. Riverdale students were nowhere to be seen since first period was about to start. When the football team came out of the gymnasium doors, it was obvious that they were just being nosy.

"Ooh, cutie alert," Brandi said, pointing their way.

Shane waved at them as a group of girls passed by in a Mercedes Benz SUV. "Go back to Po' City High!" one of them yelled.

When the football team witnessed what happened, they closed the gym door.

"What was that?" Marisa asked.

"I don't know," Brandi said as her eyebrow lifted in disapproval.

Shane never stopped taping. She walked over to the gym and banged on the door. One football player opened up in his practice pants and no shirt. "Hey, you can't tape me," he protested. "I'm not dressed."

"Boy, please. I don't care about that." She pushed past him and entered the boys' locker room. There were bodies scrambling for towels as she went in to confront them. "Not bad," she said to one guy as she passed. "Look, I'm documenting everything that goes on while we're here at Riverdale, so put the word out. The last thing you want is to tarnish your little picture-perfect image in the community. So get your people together."

There was another knock on the door. "Man, what is going on?" One of the biggest guys in the room went to open the door. "What?"

"We were ... um ... looking for," Marisa stumbled over her words. She hadn't expected boys without clothes on. *What is Shane thinking?* She covered her eyes and proceeded through the open door.

"May I?" Brandi said as she walked in and touched the boy's chiseled chest. "Niiice." She nodded her approval.

"B? Stop that!" Shane fussed. "I'm putting the rules down," she said in a stage whisper. "Behave."

"Now, like I was saying. I will be recording everything." She let her camera follow one of the guys on the team from head to toe. "It can be all good or all bad. You decide."

"Are you threatening us?" one of the guys said condescendingly.

Shane recognized him. "Hey, I know you," she said. "You're the quarterback, right?"

"Yeah, and team captain."

"Well, Mr. Captain, I'm Shane Foster, and I don't make threats. Got it?"

There was another knock on the door, and the wannabe bouncer went to open it again. "Who is it this time? How many people in this little crew?"

"Put some clothes on, child!" a lady fussed at him. "I'm the principal at PCH. I'm looking for three girls ..."

"Mrs. Montgomery? What are you doing in here?"

"No, Shane. That's my question for you," Mrs. Montgomery replied.

"I'm making a documentary about the hurricane and coping with the aftermath. I will have release papers for everyone."

Mrs. Montgomery put her hand up and slowly brought her finger to her lips. "Get back on the PCH side."

"But, Mrs. Montgomery—"

"Shane, do I have to call your father? Brandi, Marisa, are you filming too?"

"We were just leaving." There was no reason to explain. No excuse would work as to why they were in the boys' locker room while the boys were only halfway dressed.

Shane turned before she left for one last shot. "Don't forget what I said, Mr. Captain. Keep your people in line, girls and guys."

CHAPTER 16

Marisa

It was a cold and rainy day, but Marisa still needed to practice her routine for Friday night's game. When she met up with the other twirlers, she needed to have her portion of the routine down. Usually she could sneak out behind the learning trailers and practice there, but the rain was hindering that.

She tried to practice in one of the trailers, but her baton kept hitting the roof, sending it flying toward her. By the third time she got hit, she knew that she had to find another practice location.

The only place left was the girls' gym on the Riverdale campus, but that was the last place she wanted to go. With a sigh, she reluctantly gathered her things and headed toward the gym.

She walked in through the double doors and surprisingly, nobody was there. All that worrying for nothing. She turned her music on and started warming up. As she stretched, she could feel her limbs coming alive. She loved twirling. It made her feel free.

For nearly thirty minutes, she practiced her routine without interruption. She loved the changes she'd made to it. She just hoped it would blend in with what the other girls were working on. They were set to be back on the PCH field this Friday night for the first time. It was exciting and nerve-racking all at the same time.

When Marisa went to start the music over, she saw that a crowd had gathered, watching her practice. They all began clapping for her, and she could feel the blood as it rushed to her cheeks.

One girl stepped forward out of the bunch. "Well, that was just wonderful," she said, but her voice dripped with sarcasm. "Did you get permission to come over here from the trailer park?"

At first Marisa had thought their applause was sincere, but it was obviously fake. "I ... I didn't know."

"Yeah, well, you should have known." This girl was holding her baton in Marisa's face and coming closer and closer. Marisa felt threatened. The only thing she wanted was to put some distance between her and this group of alpha girls as quickly as possible. She felt like she had just landed on a different planet.

Two coaches walked into the gym as the confrontation was taking place. "Destiny, what's going on in here?" one of the coaches yelled across the gym. "And who are you?" she asked Marisa.

"I ..." Everything was happening so fast. Marisa didn't know what to say. The teacher was coming toward her. She began talking quickly. "I just needed a place to practice. It was raining outside, and the trailers are too—"

"She's a refugee!" one of the girls yelled, and they all laughed.

"That's enough!" their coach yelled. "You girls want to run today?"

"We are going to the locker room, Mrs. Daggs."

Mrs. Daggs turned her attention to Marisa. "I'm so sorry about that. Those girls were born without a sensitivity chip. Anytime you need to use the gym to practice, you are welcome to do so."

Mrs. Daggs was a breath of fresh air after that encounter. "Thanks, but I think I'll find another practice spot. I'm sure PCH will be opening back up any day now."

"Well, if not, let me know if I can do anything to help. I know it must be hard on all of you. My mother lives in Port City. She's staying with me now," Mrs. Daggs said, empathizing with her.

Marisa left the gym and went to find Shane and Brandi. She had to tell them what happened. "Where r u?" she texted her crew. They agreed to meet up in the student parking lot. There was so much to say. Marisa didn't even know where to begin. When they got in the car, Marisa began to tell them about her encounter in the gym.

"Why did you go in there alone?" Shane said, fuming. "And you let me miss all that good footage for my documentary?"

"Nobody cares about your documentary. They just pushed up on Marisa. Who is this Destiny girl anyway?" Brandi asked.

"Oh, lawd! She's the feature twirler at Riverdale," Shane said.

It was all making sense to Marisa now.

"Aw, she's cute," Brandi said, glancing at her Friender picture.

Marisa hit her in the back of the head. "Too soon! And I never said they were ugly, just mean. Hey, look at her comments. They are fussing at her for trying to go off on me."

"Trying to?" Shane questioned.

"Shut it! It was like thirty of them and one of me."

"I'm just picking on you. You know I know."

"Looks like Destiny's little beef with me blew up in her face."

"Well, at least they aren't all like that."

Marisa laughed hard. "This girl told her that she was just jealous because I was a better twirler than her." She kept reading the Riverdale gossip. "And she was at that open call for Gap."

"It's like that stalker movie where the girl wants to be the other girl. I think you have you a stalker, Mari."

"I don't know about all that, but it definitely looks like we have a lot of the same interests. She can have it all. Dance is where my heart is now."

"Really? No more modeling?"

"Modeling pays the bills and hopefully it'll pay for college too. I plan on modeling as long as I can, but it's not my life's dream anymore. I really believe that I found my calling. When I was in that play last year, my whole world opened up when I started to dance."

"It's kinda what happened to me when I joined the debate team. I love arguing my point in front of an audience. It's a great feeling," Brandi joined in.

"Yeah, maybe you'll stop arguing with us now with yo feisty behind," Shane said, still mad about the documentary comment.

"Get over yourself, Shane. Haven't I been cooperating with your little project? Taping me all the time with that phone. Just be happy about that."

Welcome to Port City, TX, the sign read on the way back to home. They were relieved. They passed by PCH just to see how far crews were getting along on the clean up.

"It doesn't look like anything has changed," Marisa complained.

"We are never coming back to our school," Brandi cried.

"Go to my house," Shane ordered Brandi. "We're going to take this up with our city councilman, my daddy."

CHAPTER 17

Friday Night Football

For the students of Port City High, the most important part of the school year was football season, but this year was different. The excitement that was usually present had disappeared when Hurricane Adam blew into town. Who could blame them? Half of the school was taking classes online while the other half was housed at Riverdale.

This was no way to start a school year. They felt displaced, and it seemed that their situation wasn't going to be changing anytime soon. After visiting the weather-beaten Port City High, Shane, Brandi, and Marisa arrived at Shane's house to speak to her father about their situation. If anybody had answers, it would be Brian Foster.

"Daddy, we have an official complaint," she told him as she walked into his home office.

"Who doesn't?" he mumbled, taking his glasses off to see his youngest daughter a little better. He looked up and her phone was pointing directly at him. "Why are you taping me, Shane?"

"It's for my documentary, Daddy. Just forget that the camera is there."

He decided to play along. "Okay. Talk to me, baby girl."

"Well, I just passed by PCH—"

"We," Brandi corrected her. "We just

passed by PCH, and we are concerned citizens."

"Are they working on it at all, Daddy?" Shane sounded more like a little girl than a concerned citizen, but her father enjoyed watching her involvement in getting her school put back together.

"What is your concern, Shane? Stick to the issue at hand." To Mr. Foster, every moment was a teachable one. There was always something that he wanted his daughters to learn from any situation. This time, he needed her to learn how to get to the point.

"My concern is that there's no progress being made at PCH, and we may never go back to our own school. We hate Riverdale. Some girls just ran up on Mari today. You know Mari is not 'bout that life," she whispered, as if that were top-secret intelligence.

"And you are? Lucky me," her father said sarcastically.

"Don't hate because I know how to carry myself," Marisa told Shane. "Rolling around in the dirt and getting in people's faces is just not my style, Mr. Foster."

"I'm not hating, Mari," Shane said. "You know better. I got your back."

"Me too," Brandi said, munching on the candy in Mr. Foster's candy dish.

"Okay, girls, first I want you to think rationally. At some point you will go back to PCH. You know that. I do have a small glimmer of hope for you, though. I just got off the phone with the mayor. He had good news and bad news."

"The only good news I want to hear is that we are going back to PCH," Marisa told him.

"Sorry, Mari, that's actually the bad news. PCH was more damaged than we thought. It's going to be some time before you're allowed to resume classes there."

"What? Daddy," Shane whined. "Well, there is no good news, then."

"Hold on, hold on. There is a silver lining. We have access to both gyms and the football field. The band hall is fine. It's just the main campus that's been compromised."

"What does that mean, Mr. Foster?" Marisa asked him.

"It means that football season is back up and running. When you leave Riverdale after classes, you can go to PCH for all your practices. The football team will have their own facilities as well. Friday night we can play at our home stadium."

They immediately began celebrating. "This is awesome, Mr. Foster. I have to get in touch with my cheerleaders." Brandi ran out of his office.

"That is definitely good news, Mr. Foster. I'm going to call the twirlers!" Marisa exclaimed.

"Well, Daddy," Shane said, turning her camera off. "I don't have anybody to call, but I'm so excited too. We need this."

"I know, baby. Now go tape their phone calls. I'll bet it would be great in your documentary," he said proudly.

"Good idea! Love you, Daddy!" She kissed his cheek and ran out of his office.

On Friday night, when they took their rightful places on their home field, it was like magic. Shane had the journalism team interviewing, filming, and documenting as much as they could. Port City had a story to tell, and they were determined to do so. News crews were outside the stadium. The whole community was rooting for the Port City Wildcats.

Shane's team of journalists was just as excited as she was about completing the documentary. As they reviewed the footage over the weeks, they realized how big their story could be. They had seen the footage from Hurricane Katrina survivors, and now they were telling their *own* story. It was going to be awesome.

The football team was winning the game against the Houston High Drillers. The PCH football players were in their zone, and they were unstoppable.

There had been big news surrounding Matthew Kincade's senior year of football. He had been on varsity since he was in the ninth grade. He was definitely living up to the hype. After Hurricane Adam, his story had become even more intriguing to the college scouts. Tonight, back on his home field, he led PCH to victory.

There was an electric current in the air as PCH students started showing up at Jerry's. They were all together again, and it was a wonderful feeling. Luckily, Shane and her team were everywhere with their cameras. If they hadn't been, then they probably would have missed all the action.

When Destiny and her friends walked into Jerry's, there was a hush over the crowd. Marisa spotted them across the room and ran over. "Get out! You are not welcome here."

"Whoa, feisty," Destiny said, putting her hand up to stop Marisa's banter. "We just came to congratulate y'all." She looked around the restaurant with her nose in the air. She and her friends looked as if bugs were crawling on the walls. "So this is where y'all hang out, huh?"

The owner of Jerry's came out. "Can we serve you anything?" he asked.

"Ew, no," Destiny answered rudely.

Brandi and Shane were by Marisa's side in no time. "What do you want, Destiny?"

"We were sent to see if the Classic was going down this year. But from the looks of this little ghost town, I just don't see it happening."

The Classic was a huge basketball event that the surrounding schools looked forward to each year. It was always hosted at Port City High. It brought the school and the city a lot of revenue. Nobody had even thought about how the storm would affect the Classic. Everybody's focus had been on football season.

"Maybe we will host this year in Riverdale."

"Over my dead body," Shane told her, getting in her face. The students in Jerry's started cheering loudly. "The Classic will be in Port City as it always is. Take that back to whoever sent you."

"I'm not afraid of you," Destiny said, looking Shane in the eyes. "Just know if you can't deliver, we will." She cocked her head to the side. "Toodles. See you all Monday. Hey, Matthew, I'll see you later tonight." She smiled mischievously as all eyes went to him.

"Hey ... I," he stumbled over his words.

Shane, Brandi, and Marisa immediately looked in Matthew's direction. He was shaking his head as though he didn't have anything to do with it, but they had enough history with Matthew to know better.

The PCH students watched as the alien invaders got into their giant Escalade and rode off into the night. They just added one more thing to their plates: getting the powers that be to organize the basketball Classic. How hard could it be?

CHAPTER 18

Shane

After their huge win over the Drillers, everyone in Port City was on the same page. It was time to get their students back to their own school. But enough money couldn't be found in the budget to make the necessary repairs to Port City High.

There was one common thread in education: schools simply did not have as much money in their reserves anymore to handle a big construction job like this one. No matter how determined they were to get back home, the money just wasn't there to make that happen.

The more Shane talked to school staff in order to get the basketball Classic going for Christmas break, the more opposition she faced. She had heard all of the excuses.

"We have other things to focus on."

"There is no money for the Classic this year, Shane. I'm sorry."

"Port City is not ready for visitors."

By the time she got to the principal's office, she was ready to fight for the Classic. She walked up the steps leading to the trailer that was designated as the administrative office. She was greeted by the secretary and allowed to go in and talk to Mrs. Montgomery.

"Shane, what a pleasant surprise," Mrs. Montgomery said. "What can I help you with today?"

"Well, Mrs. Montgomery, I've been talking to everyone who will listen about getting the Classic going."

"Shane, there's just no way. Not with our school—"

"Wait, Mrs. Montgomery. Please just hear me out." Shane took out a folder with all the teams that she had already signed up for the Classic. She had talked to the old coaches from the years before. She handed the list to Mrs. Montgomery.

"These are all the teams willing to pay to play. If we add up the money we will make from the concession stand and the money we could make from doing a raffle of some sort, we could raise enough to at least start the necessary repairs to get us back to PCH by next semester."

Mrs. Montgomery studied the data Shane had given her. "This is nice work, Shane, but I just don't know what we would need in order to ..." Her voice trailed off as if she were thinking. She began studying a spot on her desk, as if it held all the answers. Then she looked to every corner of her makeshift office. Her wheels were turning, and Shane was sure she was on board.

"You know what, Shane? Let me make some calls."

Shane was so excited. "Oh, thank you, thank you, thank you. I know we can do this. We simply can't come back here next semester. We just can't."

Mrs. Montgomery looked around. "You're right, Shane. I don't love the situation either. I think it may be time for us to take matters into our own hands, and I think this just may be the thing to do it. Nice work, very nice work."

Shane left Mrs. Montgomery's office on top of the world. She was determined to make this happen, and with Mrs. Montgomery in complete agreement, the possibilities were endless.

CHAPTER 19

Marisa

Thanksgiving break was cold and rainy. The warmth that had blown Hurricane Adam their way was now replaced by rain that froze before it touched the ground. The icicles stung the skin of those unlucky enough to have to go from place to place in such brutal weather.

The cold they felt in Port City was a joke in cities to the north. It didn't much matter what other people felt about the Texas weather. The only thing that mattered was staying out of it as much as possible.

Marisa sat in her room trying to do just that. Her mother had made a big pot of abuelita's hot chocolate and cinnamon *conchitas* for the family. The familiar aromas permeated their home, beckoning her siblings to the kitchen.

"Chocolaty conchitas," Isi said, dancing her way into the kitchen. At ten, Isi was already looking less like a little girl and more like a teenager. Her beauty was already breathtaking. Everyone said that she looked like the little version of Marisa. Marisa's modeling agent was already showing an interest in the youngest Maldonado, but their parents weren't ready for their tween to enter the modeling world. Isi begged and pleaded, but her parents were adamant about making her wait.

Her mother bought enough food when she went to the grocery store so that they could hibernate for the next week. The bitter cold kept most Port City residents in the house. The Maldonados were armed and ready to stay inside and keep busy. With a list of novellas in their queue and their favorite winter morning breakfast on their trays, they retreated to some much needed family time.

During the commercial break, Marisa headed to the kitchen to get more of her mom's cinnamon bread. *Shoot! Where did she put it?* She went to knock on her parents' bedroom door, but she could hear them in deep conversation.

"Don't worry, George. Work will open up in Port City soon. We will be fine."

"We really don't have the luxury of time, Lupe. Our bills are piling up. I have to go."

"You can't leave me again," her mother began to cry. "I barely survived the last time you were taken away."

"That was different. I was in jail. They don't let you come home when you are in jail. I will come home every weekend. I have the job already, and we need the money."

"I can't raise them alone. Romero needs his father. The girls need their father."

Marisa could hear her father crossing the room to console his wife. There was no way she would interrupt their private moment. Her mother wasn't an overly emotional person, but Marisa could hear her crying. It was hard.

Marisa walked away from the door and went back to watch the remainder of her novellas, but it wasn't the same. She loved her father. It was hard to imagine seeing him only on weekends. He was her hero.

"Get up! We have work to do!" Shane yelled into the phone.

"It's freezing outside, and I'm not leaving."

"Girl, the Classic is not going to plan itself. I need help from my besties. Brandi will be there to pick you up in twenty minutes."

"Noooo."

"Yes, this is happening, so throw on some warm-ups, your snow boots, and that cute little puffy coat. We have work to do."

Shane had already organized all of the teams for the basketball tournament. She was in the process of making the flyers, but she needed Brandi and Marisa. Brandi was good with words, and Marisa was a beast at Photoshop. Together they could produce a flyer to entice anybody to attend their event.

They worked feverishly on the flyer, only breaking for food. It was an all-day event, but well worth it. When they were done, the flyer was hot. It was sleek, fast, and inviting.

"I think my daddy's leaving," Marisa blurted out as they put the final touches on their work.

"What do you mean leaving? To go where?" Shane questioned.

"Your parents are getting a divorce?" Brandi asked in disbelief.

"Divorce, no. Where, I don't know."

"Well, how do you know he's leaving?" Shane asked her.

"I overheard my parents talking. He just can't find work here. They don't know that I know."

"I'm sorry, Marisa. I know you're nuts over your dad," Brandi told her.

"Yeah, he says he'll come home on the weekends, but I don't know ..."

It was difficult. Marisa didn't know what to say or how to feel. It was her senior year, and Hurricane Adam had torn up more than just their neighborhood and their school. Adam had come to Port City and torn up her entire life.

CHAPTER 20

Brandi

$\mathcal{B}$randi and Raven had been walking on eggshells around their mother since they had returned from Austin. Even their dad was cautious. Most of the time, she didn't pay attention to any of them, even if they were talking directly to her. When she did hear what they were saying, she was very snappy and aggressive. When Brandi's father walked in on Brandi consoling Raven after another verbal assault from her mother, he was ready to lose it.

"We can't go on like this. I've been understanding because your mom has been so understanding with me. It's getting to be too much, though." Mr. Haywood shook his head in disbelief.

"Daddy, has she told you about the night of the storm yet? Did she tell you what happened?" Brandi asked her father. "It's like it's just building up inside of her."

"No, she didn't tell me, but I know. I can understand her not wanting to talk about it. Things happened. Bad things happened and people died. I hear it was a pretty intense night." He turned his attention to his youngest daughter. "Don't cry, RaRa."

"I just wanted to tell her about my day. That's all. It's like I don't have a mother anymore."

"Baby, don't say that. Mama will be back. We just have to support her. She's going through a rough patch. The bad thing is that she was trying to do a good thing by staying at the hospital with her patients. Nobody could have anticipated that the generators would go out, or that the machines that keep people alive would have to be manually operated in some cases. You know Mommy. She jumped right in there to help, but ..." He just shook his head.

"That's so sad," Raven admitted.

"Yes, very sad, so be patient. Time heals all wounds."

He was just as worried as his daughters about his wife, but he had to put on a brave face for his girls. It was becoming apparent that Catherine Haywood was in more trouble than she let on. She had been there for him through his drug addiction and his numerous visits to rehab. He had to find a way to be there for her.

Mr. Haywood decided to enlist help from the psychiatrist at her hospital, Dr. Bartlett. They had always been friendly with one another at work functions. He knew if Dr. Bartlett couldn't help her himself, then he would point them in the right direction. When Mr. Haywood contacted the doctor, he was more than happy to help him out. Catherine Haywood had always been one of his favorite nurses.

Dr. Bartlett showed up before Mrs. Haywood could get home from work. He looked at all the family pictures on the walls as he sipped the sweet tea that Brandi had brought him from the kitchen. He heard the front door as it slammed shut.

"James!" Cat Haywood yelled. "Did you forget to put the garbage cans out again? How many times do I have to ask you?" She stopped yelling. She was face-to-face with Dr. Bartlett, who was relaxing with a fresh glass of her sweet tea. "Doctor Bartlett? How are you? What are you doing here?" she asked, confused, as he stood up to greet her.

"I asked him to come, Catherine," her husband informed her.

The more the conversation continued,

the more confused she became. "But why?"

"Catherine, James tells me that you have had a problem adjusting back to normal life since the hurricane."

"I guess you could say that." She looked at her husband and tried to read his mind. "I'm dealing with it, Doctor. James should not have asked you to come here. I'm fine."

"You didn't sound fine when you came through that door just now. If that's what your family is seeing, then he had reason to call me."

"You don't know how many times he's forgotten the garbage," she said. She was about to get defensive and caught herself.

"Yes, but there's another way to deal with that. You are on edge, Catherine. I've seen it before. It's typical in patients dealing with post-traumatic stress disorder."

"PTSD? I don't have PTSD. That's for people coming back from war."

"It's caused by a life experience that is

viewed as traumatic by an individual. It can feel like war, but it doesn't have to be. I think I can help you through this, Catherine. Please, let me try."

"Yeah, Mom. Let him try." Mrs. Haywood snapped her head to see her two daughters looking back at her. Brandi walked toward her mom. "You have to come back to us. You're lost right now," Brandi added.

"We will be here for you, Mommy. I'll clean my room and everything," Raven told her. "I won't bother you when you come home, and I'll only tell you about my day when you ask. I promise."

She looked at her husband. Her eyes filled with tears. "Has it been that bad?" None of them had the courage to answer that question. However, it didn't need an answer. Dr. Bartlett wouldn't be standing in their living room if it weren't that bad. "I don't know if I'm ready to talk about that night, Doctor. I don't know if I can do it."

"Catherine, we are all going to help you get through this. You don't have to do it alone. I can see you at the hospital, but you have to get some help. I've counseled some of the other doctors and nurses from that night, and they are getting better. Let me help you too."

She bowed her head and sobbed like a small child. She hadn't thought about all those people trying to heal. She had been so focused on her own pain. Her husband rushed to her side as she collapsed in her living room. Brandi and Raven rubbed her back, crying along with their mother. "It's okay, Mama. It's going to be okay."

"I can't get the faces of the dead out of my head. I dream about them when I'm asleep. They invade my thoughts during the day. Oh, God ..." Just as she had gone down, she straightened as if she had summoned strength from somewhere deep in her being. "Doctor, I need your help, and I'm going to take it."

"Oh, Mommy. Thank you," Raven said, hugging her tightly.

"I don't feel like I've come home since the storm." She wiped the tears from her eyes. "Don't you girls worry about me. It's my job to worry about you. With Doctor Bartlett's help, I'm going to get better. I promise."

Mrs. Haywood hugged her babies tightly. She had never thought about how this depression was affecting them. Now that she had been forced to confront her pain, she knew they were right. It was too much for them to take. They had been through enough.

CHAPTER 21

The Classic

Pulling the basketball competition together had been a lot of work, but Shane Foster had been determined to get it done. Her father loved the fire that had been ignited in his younger daughter and decided to help feed the flames. He made some calls on her behalf. Sponsorships were coming in from every direction.

The Port City High School Basketball Classic
Sponsored by:
Power-ade • Casa Grande • Zummo's

Blue Bell • Pappa's • Chick-which
Jerry's • The Room
All proceeds will go to the renovation of
Port City High School • Port City, Texas

Adding the sponsors to the flyer meant a lot to them. It meant that the businesses in the area supported their school. The city was rooting for PCH to get back on its feet. Thanks to many sponsors, the last-minute preparations had been a piece of cake. The organizers were even able to add door prizes, which had never been done before at the Classic.

With the help of Brandi and Marisa, Shane had pretty much planned the whole event by herself. It was her baby. Usually the Classic would only allow schools to participate in the competition, but she had a different plan. They allowed anyone to compete who could pull a team together and had the money to buy into the tournament.

The Classic hadn't been a priority to anybody else, but Shane knew that it would be just the thing to bring everybody together.

Shane, Brandi, and Marisa were armed and ready with their wireless headsets. They wanted to communicate with one another throughout the event.

"This is going to be the best week of our lives," Brandi said into her headset. "I just wish Dub wasn't performing for the halftime show. I can jam to his music, but I don't want to see him."

"Well, he wants to see you, Brandi. He asked me if you were going to be here," Shane warned her.

"Whatever. He's not what's up."

"Look, this is for PCH. Put your feelings aside. Y'all were over a long time ago, B."

"It's not as bad as giving Trent his own team in the tournament," Marisa joined in. "My stomach's turning flips. I haven't seen him in a year, and I don't want to."

"Ladies, get over yourselves. We talked about this already. It's not about you, Trent, Dub, or me. It's about PCH. Go, Wildcats!"

It was as if they had conjured him up. Trent Walker strolled into the gym with Dalton Broussard and two females. Marisa couldn't take her eyes off him. It was like seeing a ghost. She hated herself for still being drawn to her ex-boyfriend, but she was. She couldn't seem to help herself.

She had kept up with him on Friender, so she knew the girl who walked in with him was more than just his friend. It was an empty feeling, watching him kiss her as he retreated to the locker room where the teams met up to get their jerseys and get ready for the game.

There were eight teams in the tournament. The day before, the team captains had met at the school in order to draw numbers. Teams one and two would play against each other first. Then teams three and four, and so on. The four winning teams would play Saturday morning. The two remaining teams were scheduled for Saturday night, followed by an after-party at the Room.

Nobody could have pictured this lineup of people playing in the tournament. There were professional basketball players from Port City and Baymont. They had their own teams in the tournament. The pros acted as coaches for the games.

"How did you pull this off?" Brandi asked her through their headsets.

"To be honest with you, I don't even know." They watched as the fans cheered for their favorite players. There was a three-man team led by football star Matthew Kincade. There was a team of swimmers, track stars, teachers, and coaches. Baymont High and Riverdale High had their own teams. There were some great games.

"This is wonderful, Shane," Mrs. Montgomery told her during halftime. "I'm so happy that you talked me into this."

"Thank you, Mrs. Montgomery," she said proudly.

The tournament was more fun than anything. In the past, the teams had focused on winning, but this year it was more about having a good time and raising money. The PCH students seemed happy just to be at their home school and to not be labeled as refugees. That unpleasant word just let them know they were somewhere they didn't belong. Here it was just the opposite. They more than belonged. They ran it.

By the end of Friday night, four of the teams had been eliminated. Trent's team, Matthew's team, the Baymont team, and the PCH basketball players were still in the tournament. It had been a long, fun, and entertaining evening, but it was also exhausting.

When they were done, everybody went over to Jerry's to do what they do. It was their place to eat, talk noise, parking lot pimp, and whatever else fit their fancy. The former PCH basketball players who were in the tournament couldn't resist. It only made sense to go to Jerry's. It was tradition.

Marisa stood in the line with Isi and Nadia so they could order their food. When she noticed she had missed a call on her cell phone, she stepped outside to return it. It was from her agent, Marcie Miller.

"Marcie, I'm so sorry I missed your call," Marisa shouted over the cheerful parking lot noise.

"It's okay. I'm sorry to call so late. I have news that I had to share with you. I just received a call from *LaTeen* magazine today. And they are in love with you. Since hearing about your recovery from the accident, they want to offer you the cover."

"Are you serious? Marcie, that's awesome."

"So are you, Marisa. Now, go enjoy your Friday night. We can iron out the details next week. And, Marisa? Congratulations."

"Thank you so much." She held her phone to her heart and soaked it all in. The cover of *LaTeen*. Who would have thought?

"Good news or bad news?" she heard a familiar voice say. When she turned around, it was Trent and Dalton with their dates.

"My news ... and not ready to share."

"Hey, I'll meet y'all inside. D, give Bailey the grand tour of the Jerry's menu."

"I know how to read, Trent. I don't need a tour." She looked at Marisa from head to toe. "So you're her, huh? I thought you'd be cuter for some reason. You photograph better than you look."

"Ditto," Marisa said, shooting her

the same gaze. "Trent, I don't have time for this. I have some celebrating to do. Nobody can bring me down tonight, especially Baisey."

"It's Bailey."

"Bay, go inside. Let me talk to Marisa for a second, please." She reluctantly followed Dalton inside, but she didn't order. She stood by the window, watching them.

"You brought her to Port City? Must be getting serious."

"Nah, she's from Lake Charles. I'm just giving her a ride home. I didn't think—"

"You didn't think bringing her to the Classic was a bad idea? We organized the event! Really? And you let her disrespect?"

"Mari, I'm sorry. Dang! Look, we need to talk, but not here. Can I come and see you before I go back to school?"

"Trent, I've moved on. I don't think that's a good idea."

"Trent!" Bailey screamed from the door of Jerry's.

"Just go and leave me alone." She turned her back to him. The nerve! She was angry and sad all at the same time. She had wondered what it would be like to see him again, but she had never anticipated he would bring a girl home with him to Port City.

Shane and Brandi were by her side before Trent could get to the door.

"Hey, mami. You okay?" Brandi asked.

"I'm good. No, I'm better than good. I just got the cover of *LaTeen* magazine."

The screams could be heard inside. Her girls were jumping up and down. They thought they were coming outside to console her, but instead they were celebrating. Isi, Nadia, and Raven saw them and ran outside.

"What happened?" they were all asking at the same time.

"Your sister happened," Shane said. "Mari got the cover of *LaTeen*."

More screaming from the three little

girls. Semi-chaos. It was one of those days that couldn't be imagined. It was a day of great basketball, great news, and great friends.

They walked back into Jerry's and made the announcement. Everyone congratulated Marisa. They were so happy to see one of their own Port City girls reaching for her dreams.

Trent got up to give her a hug and kissed her on the forehead. Bailey stood up and stormed out of the restaurant. "This is what happens when you bring your hoochies on our turf. Bad idea, Trent," Shane told him.

"Um-hm, then they have to have all this fabulousness up in their faces," Brandi told him.

"You three? I've missed y'all," he admitted. "I hope you're running PCH like we taught you."

"Boy, we were running it when you were here. You see how we get down. This is just a day in the life," Shane said with a shrug.

"Well, I'll catch y'all tomorrow. I'm going to get Bailey home tonight. Can we all hang out after the game tomorrow night? I have a little surprise for all of you."

"Sure," they agreed before going their separate ways.

TRAUMATIZED

Epilogue

The last night of the Classic had been epic. It looked like everyone in Port City attended. There wasn't an empty seat in the house. They all waited anxiously to find out if they made enough money for the restoration of PCH.

When the announcement came, the gymnasium cheered. The fundraiser had gone beyond anyone's expectations. Not only was the budget made, it was exceeded. The crowd went crazy.

At halftime, there was a call for volunteers. Anyone who was willing and able could help repair the school. Surprisingly, everybody in the audience was on their feet. The number one priority of Port City residents was getting their children back in their own high school. It was thrilling to know that the school was going to open before senior year was over.

After the game, the girls met up with Trent as planned. Marisa had fussed all the way up to that point. "I don't want to hang out with Trent. I'm leaving the past where it belongs, in the past."

"I have a feeling that Trent's not your past, Mari. Call me crazy," Shane told her.

"Crazy," Marisa responded.

Now they stood outside the gym after the Classic was over, and after they had raised all the money necessary to finish their senior year at PCH. Trent drove up, blasting the new Young Dub CD that wasn't even in stores yet.

"Turn that off," Brandi protested.

"What you got against Young Dub?"

The passenger window slowly rolled down and the man himself sat in the seat.

Brandi rolled her eyes. "What the? Is Flo in the backseat too?" she asked, looking in the back. "Oh!" she said, surprised when she looked. "Is *he* the surprise?"

"What?" Shane asked, jumping to see who was there. It was Ashton, in full military gear. "Ash!" she cried. It had been more than a year since they had been face-to-face.

"Surprise!" Trent yelled out. "I thought it would be best if we all got caught up. Now, all aboard."

Ashton got out of the truck. "Hey, Shane," he said, moving the hair that was blowing over her face so he could see her better.

"What are you doing here? I heard that you were in Germany."

"I was, but I had to come back to help. When I talked to Moms, she told me how hard you were working to rebuild Port

City. There will be more guys on leave joining us for the reconstruction."

"Ash, you are amazing."

He smiled down at Shane. "No, you're the amazing one."

"Hey, let's get out of here. Dub got a suite for the night. You have new swimsuits, pj's, and we'll get whatever else you need ... or want."

"What about Bailey?" Marisa asked Trent.

"Who?" She looked at him as though he was an idiot. "Oh, Bailey. She's history."

"Your choice or hers?"

"Both. She said I didn't look at her like I looked at you. I apologized. I was sorry she noticed that. I never wanted to hurt her, but you are a hard person to stop loving, Marisa Maldonado."

Marisa melted. The defenses that she had around her heart were slowly fading. "You hurt me, Trent."

"I know, but I won't do it again. I want you to come to Arkansas with me next year."

"What? I can't."

"Don't answer me right now. Just think about it. Okay?"

"Okay, I'll think about it."

Brandi was sitting next to Young Dub in the driver's seat of Trent's truck. "B, I know you still hate me for what happened with Flo."

"I don't hate you, Dub. I was madder at me than you. I should have never fallen for a rapper. Duh."

"That's not fair. We weren't in a relationship."

"But we were working on it. You told me that there was nothing between you and Flo. You lied to me, Dub."

"I'm sorry. I know you won't forgive me overnight, but can we at least work on being friends? I miss you. I like you backstage at my concerts. I like looking into the audience and seeing you and your girls. Y'all the tightest girls in Port City anyway."

"Boy, flattery will get you everywhere. Just know we are working on our friendship, nothing more," Brandi said.

"For now."

"Let's roll out, man! We can talk about this in the Jacuzzi. Y'all still rocking those purity rings, huh?"

"You know it!" they all said proudly, pointing to their ring fingers.

"That's what I like to hear," Trent said, hugging Marisa. "Now, let's go have some fun."

And fun they had. They laughed and joked around until the sun came up. There was nothing like good friends, good fun, and no pressure. There had been enough drama in their lives, but now it was time to coast into the next chapter.

The Haywood family was in therapy together, and it was just what the doctor ordered for Catherine Haywood's PTSD recovery.

The Maldonado family was getting adjusted to their father working out of town, and it really made their weekends extra special.

The Foster family was enjoying life and each other. Brian Foster was busier than ever, working with the mayor and trying to restore the city.

Yes, they were all ready for the next phase. It was going to be a new year, and there were a lot of new adventures to look forward to. The girls were finally starting to understand why these high school years were the best days of their lives. And they were spending them just how they wanted to ... together.

Shannon Freeman

Born and raised in Port Arthur, Texas, Shannon Freeman works full time as an English teacher in her hometown. After completing college at Oral Roberts University, Freeman began her work in the classroom teaching English and oral communications. At that time, the characters of her breakout series, Port City High, began to form, but these characters would not come to life for years. An apartment fire destroyed almost all of the young teacher's worldly possessions before she could begin writing. With nothing to lose, Freeman packed up and headed to Los Angeles, California, to pursue a passion that burned within her since her youth, the entertainment industry.

Beginning in 2001, Freeman made numerous television appearances and enjoyed a rich life full of friends and hard work. In 2008, her world once again changed when she and her husband, Derrick Freeman, found out that they were expecting their first child. Freeman then made the difficult decision to return to Port Arthur and start the family that she had always wanted.

At that time, Freeman returned to the classroom, but entertaining others was still a desire that could not be quenched. Being in the classroom again inspired her to tell the story of Marisa, Shane, and

Brandi that had been evolving for almost a decade. She began to write and the Port City High series was born.

Port City High is the culmination of Freeman's life experiences, including her travels across the United States and Europe. Her stories reflect the friendships she's made across the globe. Port City High is the next breakout series for today's young adult readers. Freeman says, "The topics are relevant and life changing. I just hope that people are touched by my characters' stories as much as I am."